AUTHOR'S NOTE

is is a work of historical fiction. I have made every attempt
ensure historical accuracy. Any errors that remain are mine
ne. The characters are fictional except for the following,
order of reference or appearance: Dr. Heikki Koljonen,
r. J. F. Cooke, Archduke Franz Ferdinand of Austria,
r. W. J. Dobbie, Martin Luther, Prime Minister Robert
rden, and Robert Service.

The cities of Port Arthur and Fort William are now part of
under Bay, Ontario, on the north shore of Lake Superior.

Please see the glossary at the back of the book for a basic
ide to the pronunciation of Finnish words that appear in
is story. At the back of the book you'll also find historical
formation and photographs.

Saara's Passage

Karen Autio

For Emma,
Live on purpose.
Karen Autio

sononis
PRESS

WINLAW, BRITISH COLUMBIA

Copyright © 2008 by Karen Autio

LIBRARY AND ARCHIVES CANADA CATALOGUING IN PUBLICATION

Autio, Karen, 1958-
   Saara's passage / Karen Autio.

ISBN 978-1-55039-168-8

   I. Title.

PS8601.U85S37 2008   jC813'.6   C2008-904557-2

Sono Nis Press most gratefully acknowledges support for our publishing program provided by the Government of Canada through the Book Publishing Industry Development Program (BPIDP) and the Canada Council for the Arts, and by the Province of British Columbia through the British Columbia Arts Council and the Book Publishing Tax Credit, Ministry of Provincial Revenue.

Edited by Laura Peetoom and Dawn Loewen
Interior layout by Frances Hunter
Cover photo of girl by Doug Wilson
Cover photo of sleigh © 2008 Jeff Shultz / AlaskaStock.com

Published by   Distributed in the U.S. by
Sono Nis Press   Orca Book Publishers
Box 160   Box 468
Winlaw, BC V0G 2J0   Custer, WA 98240-0468
1-800-370-5228   1-800-210-5277

books@sononis.com
www.sononis.com

Printed and bound in Canada by Houghton Boston Printers.
Printed on acid-free paper that is forest friendly (100% post-consumer recycled paper) and has been processed chlorine free.

For Mom,
in celebration of all the yea
we had with Mummu

∼

S. D. G.

*A valuable life had been lost, and
to make up for it, I had to find value in mine.*

—AMY TAN, The Opposite of Fate: A Book of Musings

PROLOGUE

"*Leipä?*"

"That one's easy, Mummu," I said, grinning from the old pine rocking chair in the corner of my great-grandmother's bedroom. "It means 'bread.'"

"You're right, Aliisa," she said. "How about *kissa?*"

I giggled at the sound of the Finnish word. "It means 'play'—no, wait. It's 'cat.'"

Mummu nodded, her smile rearranging the wrinkles of her cheeks. She shifted in her recliner, pulling the multicoloured quilt higher over her legs. "I see you've been studying the vocabulary list I gave you."

Like a hug, the pride in her voice warmed me. "Ask me another one."

"*Yhdeksän?*"

Cringing, I silently counted up from one on my fingers. "Is it eight?"

"No, nine."

"Arrrg! Numbers are so *hard* to remember."

"Oh, Aliisa-*kulta*," said Mummu, shaking her head. "Now you remind me of Lila."

"Who's Lila?" asked Mom, entering the bedroom carrying a wooden tray. She set it down on a TV table.

The tray was loaded with a steaming teapot, mugs, spoons, milk and sugar, and cardamom cookies.

"My friend Lila lived on the farm next to Uncle's homestead in North Branch. She and Mikko endured my first attempts at teaching. It was teaching English, believe it or not, and I was only twelve!"

"After the *Empress of Ireland* sank?" I asked, stirring a heaping teaspoon of sugar into my blackcurrant tea.

"Yes. My twelfth birthday was only two days after the sinking." Mummu wore a faraway look and sighed heavily. "I was still recovering in Quebec." Her eyes turned back to me and she smiled reassuringly. "But we celebrated properly later, at home."

· Mom gingerly handed Mummu her mug, the one with the lilac design. Then she grabbed the rose mug and two cookies for herself. Nestling on the bed, she asked, "Did you live at your uncle's homestead that summer?"

A question popped up in my head, so I leaned forward and blurted, "Did you ever figure out *why* your life was spared?"

Mummu chuckled. "I'll need to tell another whole story to answer those questions."

My chair rocked back so far on its extra-long runners, I narrowly missed spilling my tea. "Go ahead, Mummu. I promise I won't interrupt."

Following a sip of milky tea, Mummu closed her eyes to concentrate. "It was June 28, 1914, when we celebrated so many happy things—my birthday, our surviving the sinking, and the arrival of my baby cousin. I had no inkling how much life would change overnight …"

1

"Keep kicking!" I cried in panic. But my brother's body went limp. The icy river sucked at us. Cold sliced through me.

The *Empress* had vanished. Would the river swallow us, too? I desperately kicked and clawed the black water. John's weight dragged at me. I tightened my grip on his hair.

Is he still alive? "John, say something!" He didn't speak, but he coughed. "Thank you, God," I whispered.

Another cough. Could he hold on long enough to be rescued?

Cough. It wasn't John's deep bark. The freezing water binding my legs became tightly wrapped bedclothes.

Cough. Cough. Awake now, I knew that sound. It was the dry yet stubborn cough of my beloved Aunt Marja, trying ever so much not to disturb anyone.

I blinked in the dawn light that peeked around my curtains. Sipu purred and uncurled herself from my side. She stretched every part of her furry grey body. Heart still racing, I clutched my cat. We were home.

John was safe. Sipu meowed and squirmed out of my grasp.

I knew it was only a dream, yet lingering fear clenched my insides. How could I shake off this horrible feeling? I had to focus on something happy … like yesterday. Our family from the country and our city friends had gathered after church to celebrate my birthday and my new baby cousin, Sanni. I'd held her for the first time. Everyone had again exclaimed over the miracle that Mama, John, and I had survived the sinking of the *Empress of Ireland* in the St. Lawrence River the previous month. As I remembered the best part of the day, my heartbeat began to slow down. Papa had come to say good night and he'd sung to me his "Saara song." He hadn't done that in months, being so preoccupied with money worries and finding a steady job.

Humming my song, I could feel my stomach relax. I decided to surprise Mama. I'd light the fire in the wood stove and set the water to boil for coffee.

It worked! By the time Mama appeared, I had finished grinding the coffee beans in the mill, too.

"Excuse me, miss, where my Saara has gone?" asked Mama. She stood in the doorway, looking the perfect picture of a fine lady surprised to find a stranger in her kitchen. I giggled, and she struggled to keep a straight face. "Saara has long blond hair in braids, is tall for twelve, and avoids kitchen work like the plague," Mama continued, switching to her usual Finnish. "I don't know what's gotten into you this morning, Saara, but it certainly has my approval."

What had gotten into me—returned to me—was the joy-bubble that had grown bigger throughout the previous day. I smiled and gathered cutlery from the drawer.

"What woke you so early," asked Mama, "another nightmare?"

When I nodded, she took a breath as if to speak. I expected one of her Finnish proverbs. Instead she simply patted the back of my head.

Mama bustled about the kitchen with only a trace of a limp. That and two scars on her face remained from her shipwreck injuries. My worst injuries—memories and fears—were stowed away inside. They were invisible but would seize me without warning, day or night, tying my stomach in knots.

We loaded the breakfast table with dark rye bread, homemade white cheese that squeaked when chewed, and a bowl of *viili* for everyone. A cast-iron pan was heating on the stove for the eggs we would fry. Thanks to our relatives' visit, we didn't have to eat porridge for once.

The coffee's aroma must have reached the second storey. I heard voices and then footsteps on the stairs.

"Good morning," said Uncle Arvo, cradling eleven-day-old Sanni.

"May I please hold her?" I asked, reaching for my cousin.

"Sit down first."

Once I was seated he placed his tiny daughter in my arms. I carefully supported her head and stroked her strawberry-blond fuzz. I marvelled at her perfectly formed miniature fingers. She was a doll come to life.

"Good morning, Marja," said Mama to her sister as she entered the kitchen. "Did you get any sleep?"

Auntie's shoulders sagged and her eyes were darkly ringed. "A little. I never imagined how much one small baby could tire a grown woman." She coughed and draped Sanni's pink and yellow patchwork quilt over the back of the chair next to mine. When Auntie sat down, Sanni stopped behaving like a doll and began to fuss. I wanted to hand her to my aunt, but Auntie looked exhausted. Instead I shifted Sanni upward with her head resting in the warm place between my shoulder and neck. Was that the right thing to do? She seemed more content, making snuffling noises against the collar of my dress.

While Mama circled the table pouring coffee into cups, John and Papa joined us. She replaced the enamel pot on the stove, looked at Papa, and asked, "Shall we say grace?"

My father attended church with us—each Sunday without fail since we'd returned from Quebec—but he never prayed out loud. Papa cleared his throat and said, "Arvo?"

Uncle closed his eyes. "Father in Heaven, we ask Thy blessing on this food and on those who prepared it. Amen."

Sanni whimpered. I jiggled her, hoping that would settle her. Before Auntie could swallow one spoonful of *viili*, Sanni began to cry. Mama must have seen the panic in my eyes because she offered to rock her.

Auntie sighed and shook her head. "Thank you for trying to soothe her, Saara. That's her hungry cry. Only her mother will do." She whisked Sanni from my arms, grabbed her quilt, and headed into the parlour to nurse her, coughing along the way.

Mama cracked eggs into the pan. Leaving them sizzling, she laid her hand on Uncle's arm and whispered, "You must persuade Marja to see Dr. Koljonen about her cough before you go home."

Papa set down his coffee. "Stop interfering. Your sister can look after herself."

"Don't fret, Emilia," said Uncle Arvo, helping himself to bread. "It's a summer cold. No wonder, with her being worn out from the birthing and caring for Sanni."

"How long has she had that cough?"

Uncle paused, staring at his meal. "Hmm … I don't know for certain. I think it started a couple of weeks before Sanni was born. Maybe three."

Mama lowered her voice so I could barely hear. Her eyes pleaded intently. I nibbled my cheese while John shovelled *viili* into his mouth. Nudging his foot, I signalled him to mind his manners. He kept on shovelling, smacking his lips to annoy me.

"Are the eggs ready?" asked Papa, holding out his plate.

I jumped up, saying, "I'll get one for you." I didn't expect him to thank me, but he did give me a smile. Mama served Uncle, John, then me.

My uncle ignored his egg and smoothed back his reddish-blond hair, deep in thought. "Marja's had a few bad colds since Christmas."

Auntie appeared in the doorway. "Thank you for your

concern. I'll be fine in no time, as soon as I get more sleep." Sanni's quilt slipped to the floor. Auntie bent over to retrieve it and staggered against the wall.

"Marja!" Mama rushed over to catch Sanni.

Uncle helped Auntie to her chair. She rubbed her forehead. "How strange. I saw stars and felt faint ..."

Her husband took her hand. "I think it *is* wise for you to see the doctor."

Mama nodded. "And you must see him today. Who knows when you'll be back in Port Arthur." Turning to me, she said, "Run down to the doctor's office and request a house call."

I swallowed the bit of rye bread in my mouth and drained my glass of milk. Outside, bees danced among the pink and white peonies. Writing the first entry in my new journal would have to wait. My best friend, Helena Pekkonen, had given the brown leather-bound journal to me at my birthday celebration. It was a duplicate of the one she'd given me for the trip to Finland, the adventure that ended before we left Canada ... the adventure that ended in tragedy. Mama, John, and I had boarded the *Empress of Ireland* heading to England. When a coal ship struck us in the night, the *Empress* sank. More than a thousand people perished.

The memory made my breathing quick and shallow, and my throat thickened as I crossed Secord Street. The two blocks to Dr. Koljonen's office on Machar Avenue were jam-packed with confectioneries and laundries, barbers and liveries, as well as the huge Finnish Labour Temple, also known as the Big Finn Hall. I shared the

14

sidewalk with half a dozen early shoppers. As I entered the doctor's office, the smell of iodine hit me full force. In a flash I was back at the Château Frontenac, a nurse bending over me to clean my wounds, the cold of the icy St. Lawrence River in my bones.

The panic I knew that dark night in the water washed over me afresh, and I had to push it back in order to see the Finnish doctor standing before me. Dr. Koljonen's white shirt sleeves were rolled up, and his necktie was loosened above his stethoscope. He asked, "How can I help you, Miss Mäki? Is Jussi sick again?"

"No, sir. My brother is well." I explained Aunt Marja's situation. "Will you be able to see her today?"

"I can come this afternoon. Tell Jussi to stay away from your aunt."

"Yes, sir. Thank you." The last thing John's weak lungs needed was a cold. I sped home.

After lunch, Auntie settled Sanni for her nap and decided to lie down until the doctor arrived. I went back outside to visit Uncle's workhorses in the shelter. Copper, the chestnut mare, and the black gelding called Ace were dozing. Each rested a hind leg, holding it on the point of the hoof. They looked so peaceful, I didn't want to disturb them. I decided to go to Helena's for a short visit instead. I would still be back in time to see Baby Sanni before she returned to the homestead in North Branch.

Dust clouds puffed around my feet as I ran down the lane. Helena waved from the shady spot beside the rain barrel in their backyard. "Come help me with the rhubarb and then we can play hopscotch." Helena's family was Finnish, too, but she and I spoke English with each other. She was a year older than I was but had been set back a grade when she arrived from Finland.

"Do you want to wash or trim?" she asked, holding out a knife.

"You know knives don't agree with me, especially your mother's razor-sharp ones." I grabbed the longest stalk from the pile on the grass, dipped it in the basin of water, and rubbed off the dark earth. "In this heat I'd rather jump in the swimming pool at Current River Park than play hopscotch."

"That's a terrific idea. All we need are a couple of nickels for streetcar fare—"

"I need more than coins," I said, sighing and reaching for another reddish-green stalk. "I've outgrown my bathing suit and money is so tight I don't know when I'll get a new one."

"Cheer up, gloomy goose. You don't need a bathing suit to come to the Dominion Day events with us on Wednesday."

"Your father said yes? Hurrah!"

"We'll bring a picnic lunch, too." Helena sliced the big rubbery leaf off a rhubarb stalk. "I clipped a recipe from the Home Loving Hearts section in the *Free Press* for Perfect Picnic Sandwiches and we'll have devilled eggs and—"

I flung a handful of rainwater at Helena.

"Hey—what's that for?"

"You sound like an uppity English lady planning your

'*Perfect* Outing in the Park,'" I said, using a British accent for the last phrase. "Don't forget we haven't grown up yet."

Helena scooped water with both palms together and threw it at me. I gasped. She'd soaked the whole front of my light cotton dress. I returned the favour. Within seconds we were both drenched and collapsed on the grass, giggling.

"Are you ready for hopscotch now?" she asked.

Tilting my head and fluttering my eyelashes, I said, "I feel *perfectly* refreshed, my dear. It would be a *pleasure* to join you—" Helena aimed the water right at my mouth this time. I took the hint and stopped teasing. "Come on," I said, reaching for her hand. "After a game of hopscotch, let's practise for the Dominion Day foot races."

By the time I returned home, it was after four o'clock. Dr. Koljonen had come and gone. Auntie, Uncle, and Sanni had already left for the farm. *Drat.*

Mama kept unusually quiet throughout cooking supper. When we sat down to eat, John began chattering. "Fred got a set of Meccano and he let me play with it. Guess what we made? It was bully! We fastened the strips together with the nuts and bolts and made a train track from one end of his bedroom to—"

"Jussi, stop," said Papa. "We've heard enough. Eat your food." What was bothering Papa? He always wanted to hear about John's day.

Later, as I stood at the sink, hands deep in steamy dishwater, Mama told Papa that Auntie might need to go to Toronto. Could I have heard right? Yes, she said it again. Why Toronto? It was almost a thousand miles from Port Arthur.

Toronto was where Mr. Blackwell lived. We'd met the Salvation Army soldier on the pier before boarding the *Empress of Ireland*. I'd become fast friends with his daughter, Lucy-Jane. We'd played in the third-class indoor children's playground and planned to spend all our time on the voyage together. That evening we'd shared our single meal on the ship with the Blackwells.

I kept Mr. Blackwell's letter in my top dresser drawer. The thought of its horrible news still made me shudder. Lucy-Jane had drowned when the *Empress* sank. I often reread the last part of her father's letter, where he'd written these comforting words: *I believe there is a reason for all things. Sarah, your life has been spared for a purpose.*

I heaved a giant sigh. So far, the only purpose I could see for my life was washing dishes and peeling potatoes.

With Papa settled in the parlour to read the newspaper, I asked Mama, "What did you mean about Toronto?"

"Aunt Marja's cough—"

"—is a summer cold, Uncle said. So why must she go so far away?"

"Saara, the doctor doesn't believe it's a cold." Mama's face looked as pale as winter cream. "He thinks it's tuberculosis and she must be isolated. He'll have the results of her sputum test tonight, but they couldn't wait. The cows needed milking."

"When will Auntie know?"

"Dr. Koljonen will tell her on Dominion Day. He had already planned to look at land in North Branch."

"And if it is tuberculosis …"

"Marja will be sent to the sanatorium in Toronto."

In a hushed tone, I said, "I didn't know Auntie had a liquor problem."

Mama's jaw dropped. "She doesn't. Why—"

"Is it tobacco? Tuberculosis means the lungs are sick, doesn't it?"

"Well, yes, but why do you think Marja has a *tobacco* problem?"

My cheeks flared as if I were in a sauna. I swiped the back of my hand across my sweaty forehead. "I … I thought a sanatorium was for curing liquor and tobacco habits … you know, like the one on Nelson Street."

Mama thumped her hand against her chest. "Oh, Saara. That's a *sanitarium*. It's completely different." She half smiled at my embarrassment, then looked troubled once again.

"Why can't she go to the Isolation Hospital here?" I asked.

"That hospital is for scarlet fever, measles, and mumps. No, a sanatorium is where tuberculosis is treated." Mama's shoulders slumped. "If you can call it treatment. I hope and pray the doctor is mistaken."

Twinges of dread snaked through my stomach, but I told myself that Mama always worried far too much. It was impossible. Auntie didn't seem seriously ill at all.

The first day of July—Dominion Day—began with a sky full of angry grey clouds. I raced through my chores, anxious to get to Helena's. When I banged on the Pekkonens' back door, Helena's mother appeared, her cheeks flushed and apron dusted with flour. The smell of frying pancakes made my mouth water even though I'd already eaten porridge.

"Saara—you're early." She spun on her heel and darted to the wood stove to flip thin golden-brown pancakes. "Helena, set another place."

I followed my friend into the dining room crammed with hungry boarders and whispered, "Didn't you tell me to come at eight o'clock?"

"Yes, but we're leaving later than I thought," Helena said. "When Mama saw the program in the newspaper, she decided the callithumpian parade would be too boisterous for Baby Mandi. I suggested we stuff cotton in her ears, but Mama wouldn't hear of it."

Last year's callithumpian parade had indeed been a noisy affair, with marching brass bands, lavish floats, and decorated bicycles and pony carts. It was exciting, but I wouldn't mind if we missed it this year. My heart was set on running ... and winning. *Perhaps my purpose is to be a champion runner.* "Will we get there in time for the afternoon foot races?" I asked.

"Yes." Helena added a serving spoon to each large bowl of stewed rhubarb. "My father's determined to see the lacrosse match this morning." Giggling, she sputtered, "And of course we have our Perfect Picnic lunch."

I grinned, relieved. It was a long trip by electric streetcar to the neighbouring city of Fort William, but if we made it in time for the lacrosse game, we wouldn't miss the races.

After breakfast I helped clean up. Finally Helena, her parents, her sister, and I set out on the streetcar. I dropped a nickel in the cash box and patted my dress pocket. My remaining nickels were tucked in the coin purse John had given me for my birthday, alongside two pieces of Coca-Cola gum. As the streetcar rolled and swayed down the tracks, my mind turned to Auntie. I refused to worry about her. Nothing bad would happen—it couldn't. Sanni needed her.

After changing to the Fort William streetcar, we finally trundled into the city centre. We climbed down and walked to Arena Park.

"Listen—the lacrosse game has started," said Mr. Pekkonen. He took over pushing the carriage so that we could hurry. We squeezed through the crowd to get a view of the field.

One of the Port Arthur players scored, making it a

3–3 game. A loud cheer erupted from the spectators. Our team was well matched against the home team. I found it hard to keep track of the lacrosse ball as it flew between players. How did they catch it while running at such tremendous speed? The crowd gave a thunderous roar as Fort William pulled ahead by a goal. The clouds vanished, giving way to the sun. When Port Arthur scored again, we clapped and screamed, "Hurrah!" The game ended with the score tied 4–4.

"What an exciting match," said Mr. Pekkonen, mopping his sweaty brow with his handkerchief. "Too bad we didn't score once more."

The day was ideal for foot races and I itched to run. Last year, I had missed the prizes by one place. Now I was twelve, at the top of my age category. I knew I could win the race—a victory for Port Arthur!

Helena unpacked our lunch. She'd kept her promise about the Perfect Picnic: devilled eggs and delicious sandwiches, plus *pulla* and ginger cookies. But, as good as it tasted, I willed myself to eat a small amount. Never again would I race with a stuffed belly. I'd done that at the last church picnic and lost my lunch in the bushes.

I untied six-month-old Mandi's bib while her mother wiped the mushy cereal from the baby's mouth and cheeks. Mrs. Pekkonen said, "I hoped your family would join us, Saara. Yesterday your mother said she had no interest in celebrating the holiday this year. Is something wrong?"

Mandi gripped my finger and pulled it toward her mouth. I sighed. "Mama's a little concerned because Aunt Marja might have tuberculosis—"

Mrs. Pekkonen snatched Mandi's hand away from me. "Have *you* been checked by the doctor?"

I was startled by her reaction. "Yes, I was examined. Mama, Papa, and John were, too. None of us has it."

"That's a relief. Dear Marja. What a terrible shame. *Another* Finlander with the White Plague."

And *another* worrywart. Firmly, I said, "Dr. Koljonen is in North Branch today and will tell her the results of her test. *If* she has it, she'll have to go to the sanatorium in Toronto for a while, but she's going to be all right."

Mrs. Pekkonen shook her head. "Poor, poor Marja. And with a brand new baby."

"Now don't get carried away," said her husband, "or you'll scare Saara. Perhaps it's a mild case."

"As far as I've heard, they don't send mild cases to Toronto. If it could be cured at home, they wouldn't go to the expense of the sanatorium stay."

Expense? How would Uncle Arvo pay? "How much does it cost?" I asked.

"A fair amount, but it's 'pay what you can.'"

Helena reached for my hand, saying, "I hope your auntie will be well soon."

"Of course she will." I brushed the crumbs off my dress. "Let's go, Helena. The boys' races are over."

We joined girls of various shapes and sizes who'd gathered at the end of the field. A man wearing a straw hat held a megaphone to his lips. "The first contest of the day for girls will be a fifty-yard foot race for ages six and under, the second for ages seven to eleven."

Eleven? They had changed the age groupings. I wanted to protest. Last year it had been seven to twelve.

"Thirdly, there will be a seventy-five-yard race for girls twelve to fourteen."

Drat. I had to compete in the older group.

The man with the megaphone blatted, "All those intending to run in these foot races, please proceed to the starting line."

Helena smiled. "We get to race together again."

I groaned. "Once he shouts *go* you won't see me—I'll be last." I began chewing the end of one braid. As soon as I noticed, I spat it out. I had to stop that childish habit. *Maybe I shouldn't enter the race.* Imagining the other girls blasting past me, I started chewing my fingernails.

Hold on. That was the old Saara talking. The one from before the *Empress of Ireland.* Yes, the other girls were all older and had longer legs. But *I* was the girl who out-swam death.

We clapped for the younger racers. I envied the winners, each clutching a box of chocolates.

"All right, Helena. It's our turn." Under my breath I added, "Prize chocolates, here I come." I could already taste their smooth, rich sweetness.

Assembled at the start, we waited for the finish line markers to be moved twenty-five yards farther away. My stomach felt queasy. I'd never raced this distance. *Until a month ago, you never had to swim for your life in dark freezing water,* I told myself.

The starter called us to line up. When he decided we were ready, he yelled, "On your mark, get set, GO!"

Helena and I burst into stride. We kept pace with the rest of the girls, except for two racers in the lead. They had powerful legs, but they seemed self-conscious, barely swinging their arms. Thankful for the extra-roomy skirt Mama had made for my dress, I pumped my arms and gained ground. My coin purse bumped my thigh each time I swung my right leg forward.

By the fifty-yard mark, my legs burned with the strain. I was getting tired, but I refused to quit. If I pushed myself harder, I could catch up. In the last few yards I squeaked past the leading girls and crossed the finish line first. I'd done it!

Helena grabbed me in a bear hug. She was gulping air. "Con ... grat ... u ... lations."

I puffed out in return, "Thank ... you."

The man with the straw hat asked for my name and address and held out a flat box. Through his megaphone he announced, "The first-place prize, valued at two dollars and twenty-five cents, donated by Mr. J. F. Cooke, is awarded to Saara Mäki of Port Arthur. Well done."

Grinning, I accepted my chocolates, marvelling at how thin they must be. With my mouth watering, I ripped open the box. *Oh, no.* There was not one speck of sugar or cocoa inside. It held an ugly bronze mirror. My reddened disappointed face stared back at me.

"It's beautiful," said Helena. "May I hold it?"

One thing about my best friend I couldn't figure out was her preoccupation with mirrors. Did she think her nose would swell or her eyes change colour if she didn't inspect her face several times a day? I thrust the useless trinket at her and almost told her to keep it. It *was* my prize for winning, however, so I thought I ought to show it to my parents.

"Unusual form, Saara," said Mr. Pekkonen. "Nothing Olympian about it, but it won you the race." He clasped my hand and shook it, saying, "Congratulations."

"Thank you." Had I truly looked that odd? I needed to work on my form to run like a champion.

"We'll stay for the greased pig event, then head home," he said.

We found Helena's mother and sister in the grandstand and took our seats. After I offered Helena a piece of Coca-Cola gum and popped the other piece in my mouth, I lifted Mandi onto my lap. Sixty or so young men milled about the field. A cheer rose up as the pig was set loose. The porker charged through the group of men, its body slathered with grease. Each time a man's arms circled the pig trying to catch it, it squealed in terror and sped away.

Helena giggled and said, "Papa, why don't you try? They need help out there."

Mr. Pekkonen laughed. He pointed to a contestant running near the pig and said, "He's got a hold."

With a sharp twist the animal slipped out of reach, but the man grabbed its tail. Before he could slow the pig, the man tripped and let go, planting his face in the dirt.

"Aw," called the crowd with one voice. I shook with laughter, making Baby Mandi chuckle. How long could this porker escape capture?

After keeping to one end of the grounds, the pig veered toward the opposite end. It headed directly for the

Port Arthur City Band's instruments, stored in a corner of the field. The entire grandstand gasped. I swallowed my gum by accident. The frightened pig's squeals took on a higher pitch as it scrambled over brass euphoniums and trombones. As a finale, it jumped onto the big bass drum, crashing through its taut drum skin.

And then I could no longer see the greased pig and scattered instruments. A terrible image overcame me: the Salvation Army bandsmen and their instruments trapped in the *Empress of Ireland* at the bottom of the St. Lawrence River.

I shivered despite the heat and squinched my eyes shut.

3

By the following afternoon, lightning crackled and flashed against the steel-coloured sky. Mama was peering out the kitchen window after setting the used coffee cups in the sink. She wrapped her arms around herself, saying, "I wonder what the doctor told Marja."

I wasn't anxious. In fact, I was counting on the doctor's news being good. Auntie would not have tuberculosis and I could go to the homestead to be with her, Uncle Arvo, and Baby Sanni. I'd spend the whole next month on the farm with them.

Last summer my stay there had been filled with laughter. I loved looking after the workhorses and picking strawberries with Auntie. I also had fun with my friend Lila Koski, who lived on the neighbouring farm. Lila had written me a letter when she heard I might come again. She was excited for me to meet her fourteen-year-old cousin, Mikko. He and his father had recently moved into the original homestead house on the Koskis' property. With relatives to help on the farm, the Koskis had let their hired men go. *If Mikko wasn't my cousin I'd marry him,* she'd written. Reading that made my eyes roll. Another friend had gone dippy.

Mama returned to her sewing upstairs while I started washing the dishes. Thunder rumbled. Raindrops blew against the window and splattered the dry lane. Dark patches expanded in the sand.

A short while later there was a brisk knocking at the door. I dashed to answer it. There was Uncle! The pelting rain had drowned out the sound of his wagon.

"Sanni is chilled," he said, holding out their bundled baby. "Take her into the kitchen to warm her."

I gathered my cousin in my arms and hurried back to the kitchen. "Mama! Uncle and Auntie are here!"

Mama rushed down the stairs. "Oh, God, no," she whispered as she hurried out to see her sister.

Once I removed the wet outer blanket, Sanni's soft skin felt damp and cool to my touch. I wrapped a thick flannelette sheet around her and sat on a wooden chair near the stove.

Papa and Uncle carted suitcases, baskets, and bundles through to the parlour in complete silence. Was someone sobbing in the porch? Was it certain Auntie had tuberculosis? I focused on warming Sanni, snugging the sheet around her.

Mama ushered Auntie into the kitchen. I looked up to say hello, but the stark white mask over Auntie's mouth and nose stopped me cold. Tears brimmed in her eyes. Mama arranged another chair by the stove for her, opposite mine. I stared at the white mesh of the cheesecloth mask, then shifted my eyes away, before I was noticed and dismissed for being rude. I wanted to hear the grown-ups talk.

Aunt Marja took a ragged breath. "I didn't need the results of the test to know. I have a fever now and can feel my lungs waging war …" Her mask-muffled voice trailed off to nothing.

"You must follow the doctor's orders so your body can heal," said Mama.

"I told him I could rest at home—"

"Marja, you know there's no end to work as a farm wife. You won't take complete rest unless you're in the sanatorium. They will take good care of you there."

Disappointment triple-punched me in the stomach. Auntie *did* have tuberculosis. Uncle would take her to Toronto, after all. There would be no time at the homestead for me.

"The only blessing," said Aunt Marja, "is that Arvo and Sanni are clear." She wept, pressing her handkerchief to her eyes. "But my baby," she said in a broken whisper. "I wish I could bring her with me." She coughed and looked at Mama. "But I'd never forgive myself if I infected her."

Sanni couldn't go with her to Toronto? When Uncle Arvo returned from getting her settled there, how could he look after a baby *and* do the farm work?

"There's no need to fret over Sanni while you're away," said Mama. "We'll take good care of her." Mama glanced my way. "Right, Saara?"

"Oh, yes, Mama. I've always wanted a baby sister. This will be fun." I rocked Sanni in my arms. Although Auntie's mouth was hidden, her eyes told me she was smiling.

Papa and Uncle Arvo joined us. Mama busied herself making coffee.

"Dr. Koljonen wants Marja in the sanatorium as soon as possible, so we'll have to take the morning train," said Uncle. "Tauno, will you look after my horses while I'm gone?"

Papa answered, "Of course."

"The doctor said my cows should be tested for tuberculosis, since so many children get the disease from an infected cow's milk," said Uncle. "There's no sign of sickness in the herd, but I arranged for testing next week."

"Does any of their milk taste off?" asked Papa.

"No, but it can taste and look normal and still carry bovine tuberculosis."

"Who's looking after the farm while you take Auntie to Toronto?" I asked.

"Mr. Koski offered that he and his nephew would do that." The nephew must be Lila's cousin Mikko.

Auntie took a shuddery breath. "When we first saw Dr. Koljonen, he told me I had to stop nursing Sanni. So I've been pasteurizing cow's milk—heating it longer than five minutes, to be safe."

Mama nodded. "We'll do the same. To be safe."

Auntie pointed to her satchel and Uncle pulled out a package wrapped in brown paper and tied with string. Sliding the string off one corner, he unfolded the paper to reveal a photograph of Marja, Sanni, and himself.

"For you," he said, handing it to Mama. "You understand, don't you? We wanted a family portrait done ..." He swallowed hard. "... just in case."

He was infected with worry, too. It tried to worm its way inside me, but I was determined to resist.

In the morning, I followed Uncle Arvo outside. Copper nickered from the shelter she and Ace shared. We harnessed the workhorses and hitched them to the wagon. I missed Uncle's winks and teasing. He told no jokes. In fact, he said nothing. When it was time for Papa to take Auntie and Uncle to the Canadian Pacific Railway station, I climbed into the back of the wagon.

"I'm sorry, Saara," said Auntie in a ragged voice. "I think it's best to say our farewells here." She wept.

Mama held Sanni and her eyes shone with tears. "I want to embrace you, Marja, but …"

"I know … I understand," said Auntie.

"Fare thee well, dear sister."

Suddenly I remembered my bronze mirror. "Wait—I have something for you." I tore inside, past John snitching a piece of leftover bacon, and upstairs to my bedroom. I grabbed my prize and clattered down the stairs. Catching my breath outside, I reached the mirror up to Auntie. It glowed in the sunlight. "I won this … in a foot race."

"You are a kind and generous girl, Saara. Thank you." She glanced at her baby, saying softly to me, "I don't want her to be a heavy burden for your mama. Promise me you'll help look after Sanni."

How could such a sweet doll be a burden? "I promise. Get better, Auntie, and come home soon." She was crying. I watched the wagon until it rounded the corner onto Foley Street and rolled out of sight.

Over the next few days I divided my time between Uncle's horses and Sanni. Playing with her was fun—until she became cranky or drool covered or smelly. Then I turned her over to Mama. But on Tuesday Mama had a sewing job to complete and my cousin was out of sorts.

"Sanni needs a walk," said Mama. "Take Jussi with you, too."

John groaned. "Do I *have* to go? I promise I won't interrupt you anymore."

Mama shooed us away. I muttered under my breath and tucked Her Fussiness—howling—into our old wicker baby carriage. "You push," I said to John.

"I'm not pushing the carriage. That's your job."

We bounced up the short rutted lane to Banning Street. A squirrel scolded us from a tall spruce tree as we trundled over to Bay Street. Sanni stopped crying. I peeked at her every few steps to make sure she was all right. She slowly blinked, and fell asleep as we headed downhill toward Helena's house.

After seeing the grandeur of Montreal and the city of

Quebec on our trip, I found Port Arthur squat and simple. The wooden houses in our neighbourhood were set like gradual steps dotting the slope. They were plain, yet their familiarity was comforting. My eyes were always drawn to Lake Superior and across Thunder Bay to the Sleeping Giant, a rocky peninsula shaped like an Indian brave. I had a special lookout spot with a broad view of the lake, islands, and Sleeping Giant. It was my favourite place to think in private, but Sanni and the horses were keeping me so busy that I hadn't visited it in a while.

At the Pekkonens' boarding house, I said, "Let's see if Helena and Mandi can join us." John shrugged and chucked a pebble across the street. I parked the carriage on a shady, level spot of grass at the front, then leaped the steps by twos. Helena's head sprang up from her stitching when she saw me through the parlour window. She tossed aside her embroidery hoop and opened the door. "Saara—only our boarders use this entrance. What are you doing here?"

"I have Baby Sanni in our carriage," I said, pointing down the steps. "Can you and Mandi come for a walk?"

Mrs. Pekkonen appeared, balancing Helena's sister on her hip. Mandi gurgled and cooed, her bright eyes taking in the world. She returned my big smile. They followed me down the steps to ooh and aah over my cousin.

While Helena brought Mandi's carriage around, her mother asked, "Any word about Marja?"

"No. Uncle Arvo said he'd be back in a week. He doesn't want to leave the farm in his neighbours' care longer than that." I hoped Auntie would return with him.

Soon we were underway. One of my wheels began to squeak. I would ask Papa to oil it. We strolled along Algoma Street to South Ward Public School. John scooted onto the playground. He ran lengths, kicking a pine cone, while the rest of us carried on around the edge of the property.

I checked Sanni so often, Helena grew exasperated. "She's sleeping. Let her be."

I called to John and we carried on with our walk. I was relieved there was no sign of Richard outside his house on Secord Street. Every year since Junior First he'd been in my class. His constant teasing irked me, and he never let me forget my mistakes. I preferred to avoid him.

John caught up with us before we reached Bay Street. As we passed the Co-Op grocery store, the door swung open and Richard appeared.

"What's this? School's out and you two have turned into domestics?" Richard guffawed, shifting the packages in his arms.

"What's this?" I asked. "School's out and you've turned into an errand boy?" I noted with satisfaction that I'd actually made him blush.

"Hello there, John," said Richard.

"Hello," said my brother.

Helena simpered, "Did you hear that Saara won a Dominion Day foot race?"

A blush rose on my cheeks as Richard's attention shifted back to me.

"So *that's* why you bolted from school during your

Empire Day recitation," taunted Richard, laughing. "You were practising for a race."

Why did he have to bring up that fiasco? My head felt on fire as I remembered how I'd forgotten my lines at the assembly for the entire school. I jolted the squeaky carriage forward.

"Richard, can you oil that wheel for Saara?" asked Helena.

"Sure. I can borrow the oil can from the bread wagon driver," said Richard.

"No, thank you," I said.

Helena grabbed my arm. "Why not let him fix the wheel? The annoying screech is bound to wake up Sanni."

"Oh, fine."

Richard set down the groceries and headed toward Kivelä Bakery. John trotted after him.

Helena sighed. "What's wrong with you, Saara? He was teasing. It's obvious he's sweet on you."

I made a face and said, "Don't make me throw up."

The boys returned and Richard squirted drops of oil on my carriage axles, then Helena's.

"Thank you," said Helena.

"Richard says there's really going to be a war!" John exclaimed.

Richard patted him on the back and pointed at the bakery. "We heard an old-timer say with the Austrian archduke getting shot it could tip the scales in favour of war."

"Bully!" exclaimed John. His eagerness for war disturbed me.

"'Fire from a spark, war from a word' is what they say in the Old Country," I said, remembering my mother's current favourite proverb.

"If Canada goes to war, my brother will enlist," said Richard.

"Gordon's only seventeen, isn't he?" I asked.

"But he looks eighteen and he's determined to be a hero."

Helena said, "My father's set on going, too. My mother is furious."

John frowned and said, "My father won't go unless he's con- … con- …"

"Conscripted," I said. "Speaking of going, we need to get these babies home for their next feeding. John, return the oil can." He stuck out his tongue at me but did as I said.

"Goodbye, Richard," I said crisply and marched toward home. Sanni began to fret. It truly *was* time to get her back to Mama.

With Sanni in Mama's care, I retreated to the horses. Ace was so tall—seventeen hands—that I had to stand on a stool to groom him. Copper was a hand shorter, so by stretching I could brush her all over. As my rhythmic strokes freed the dust from Copper's coat, I wondered what was happening to Auntie far away in Toronto.

Uncle Arvo returned from Toronto four days later, alone.

"How is Marja?" asked Mama, serving coffee to him and milk to me and John.

"Fair. Getting bored." He slumped forward, elbows on the kitchen table. "After the sanatorium doctor examined her, he explained her condition to us. But he spoke English so fast and fancy, I couldn't catch many words." Uncle rubbed his temples. "There were many immigrant patients, but no Finlanders to translate for us. The other Finnish patients must be at different sanatoriums."

Chiding myself for thinking Auntie would be cured in a week, I asked, "How long will Auntie need to stay there?"

"I have no idea."

Since tuberculosis struck our family, I had been noticing articles about the disease in the *Port Arthur Daily News*. "Is it true they make sanatorium patients eat raw eggs?"

"Ew!" said John, wrinkling his face in disgust.

"Marja didn't mention raw eggs," replied Uncle, grimacing. "I was limited to afternoon visits, so I never saw her eating. She raved about the nutritious meals and large servings. But she also complained about having to eat lying down."

"Consumption is the same as tuberculosis, right?" I asked. Both adults nodded. "I've seen advertisements for Piso's Cure for Consumption and Doctor Barnham's Pink Pills for Pale People and Allen's Lung Balsam. We should buy these cures and send them—"

"Marja doesn't need quack doctors and fake medicines," said Mama.

"How do you know they're fa—"

"Hush, Saara."

Uncle left for the farm as soon as he finished his second cup of coffee. I would miss looking after Ace and Copper. Mama let out a most unladylike yawn. Sanni had kept her up most of the night. She handed the baby to me. "Her diaper needs changing."

"But Helena invited me to go roller skating!" One of the Pekkonens' boarders spoiled Helena like a favourite niece, giving her pocket money. She was generous enough to share so that I could roller skate for the first time.

"You're not going today. You need to watch Sanni so I can have a nap."

"Not again." I sighed loudly. "I've done that three days in a row." Was I going to miss out on fun all summer because of Sanni?

Mama yawned again. "All right. As soon as you've got Sanni napping, you can go. But I expect you to help later."

Of course the diaper wasn't just wet. I almost fainted from the stench. Horses' droppings didn't smell as bad. There was no doubt I'd rather muck out Ace's stall than deal with Sanni's "outhouse pants." If I could do the chore from a shovel's distance away it would spare my nostrils. *God, please heal Auntie real soon so I won't have to do this disgusting chore much longer.* I hurried to pin a fresh diaper in place. I tucked Sanni in the carriage parked in the shade beside the porch.

At the Lake City Rink, Helena handed me a pair of rented roller skates. Each metal plate had four tiny wheels. I slid my shoes into the clips, tightened the straps, and tentatively stood. It was easy to balance and walk. The dozens of roller skaters circled the rink with ease. I stepped out to join them and pushed off, thinking, *This is simple—like ice skating.*

But when I turned to grin at my best friend, my left roller skate veered into my right one. The clips caught and both feet flew out from under me. I landed with a thud on my tailbone. "Ow!" I wasn't sure I could stand.

Giggles erupted behind me. Senja and Edith. Of all people to see me fall, why did it have to be them? I groaned, more from embarrassment than pain, and accepted Helena's outstretched hands to pull me up.

"How did you like the view from the floor, Saara?" jeered Senja, skating off with Edith in tow.

"I fell like that my first time," said Helena. "That was when Senja and I were 'friends' and I'd invited her here. She laughed at me and left me to struggle back up. Here, hold on to me."

I linked my arm in hers. In the spring, Senja had tried to steal Helena from me and ruin our friendship. Thank goodness she'd failed.

Helena smiled. "Once around the rink and you'll be flying."

"That was quite a crash." It was Richard. I dreaded the teasing in the months to come about my fall. His brother, Gordon, rolled up beside us. He did look older than seventeen.

"Gordon," said Helena, "Richard told us you're going to sign up if there's a war."

"You're darned right—I don't want to miss the action." His chest puffed out. "They say the fighting will be over

40

by Christmas, so I want to be in the first battalion."

"Gosh, you're brave."

Uh-oh. Helena was using her sweet drool-over-the-boys tone. "We had better go," I said, pulling Helena with me into the flow of roller skaters. I focused on staying upright. We circled the rink at least a hundred times before my legs began shaking and I had to quit.

Helena and I trudged homeward. At the Star Livery, I intended to say hello to my favourite stable horse, Chief. As we approached, a shiny black automobile sped past and swerved to the side of the road. It jerked and sputtered to a stop. The driver turned around and called, "Miss Saara!"

It was Chief's groom. "Elias? I never thought I'd see you driving anything but a horse."

He chuckled. "Now that the livery has started hirin' out automobiles, they're teachin' me to drive and repair them. Can I give you young ladies a ride?"

Helena gripped my arm and whispered, "Saara, we shouldn't."

Although a ride up the hill would have been welcome, his rough driving made me nervous. "No, thank you. We're fine walking."

"Another time. Goodbye, ladies." He revved the automobile's engine and roared away, narrowly missing the utility pole.

"I'd say Elias has a few things to learn yet," said Helena. I made a wry face and nodded in agreement.

When we reached the gate to her backyard, I said, "Roller skating was great fun. Thank you."

"You caught on well. See you tomorrow." Helena opened the gate and waved goodbye.

I swatted mosquitoes away as I limped up the back lane and around the corner of the porch. Sanni mewled from the carriage. Why had Mama let her sleep the whole time I was roller skating? She wanted Sanni to sleep more at night than during the day.

As I stooped to pick up my cousin, my heart skipped a beat. Angry red spots covered her face. *Please, God, not measles.* What if we had to send Sanni to the Isolation Hospital? "Mama!" I called, bursting into the house.

"What is it?" said Mama in a groggy voice. She must have fallen asleep on the sofa.

"Sanni's sick." I thrust her at Mama, who sat up.

She inspected Sanni's face. "Did you cover the carriage with a sheet?"

"No. I thought she'd get too hot."

"She needs Zam-Buk."

"Does that cure measles?"

Mama shook her head. "No, but it stops the stinging and itching of mosquito bites."

I fetched the tin of Zam-Buk and held it open while Mama dabbed the thick green ointment on the swollen spots. "Saara, you must pay attention to every detail with a baby," she scolded. "They cannot defend themselves."

"I'll try to be more careful."

"I was thinking of moving Sanni's cradle into your bedroom and having you get up in the night with her."

Mama sounded both hopeful and doubtful, awaiting my reaction. She had taught me how to warm the milk and feed Sanni her bottle, and I wanted to make up for the mosquito bites. "I can do that, Mama."

At bedtime my confidence remained strong. How strange, though, to have a sleeping baby beside my bed. I lay awake for ages, listening to Sanni's snuffling. It seemed like only a moment later that she whimpered, yet my room was in darkness. My hand fumbled for the cradle to rock it. We soon fell asleep.

The next time Sanni made noise, it was a cry. I was in the middle of a rare pleasant dream, so I snuggled farther down my bed and covered my head with my pillow. Perhaps Sanni would stop crying after a while. I pulled my pillow down harder over my ears as the bawling grew louder, and then Sanni's crying changed to a muffled hiccupy noise. "There, there, little one," crooned Mama.

Mama? What was she doing in my room? Tossing back my pillow and covers, I leaped out of bed in time to see the back of Mama's white nightdress as she walked out with Sanni. *Drat.* Why hadn't I gotten up when I heard my cousin? I followed them to the stairs, hearing Papa muttering and turning in bed. I passed John in the hallway, rubbing his eyes, and told him to go back to sleep.

In the kitchen, Mama placed Sanni in my arms. She didn't speak, but her forceful actions as she heated the milk said everything. Mama was cross with me. I had failed to give her the extra sleep she needed. She returned to bed while I was feeding Sanni.

Come morning, the house was full of grumpy people, and Mama was still angry. "That was worse than if I'd gotten up with her in the first place," she said.

I tried to apologize, but she cut me off. "I am disappointed in you. 'When thinking of yourself, you have no time for others.'"

Over his steaming coffee, Papa scowled at me. "I thought you were becoming responsible."

My spirits plummeted. I was even more disappointed than Papa was in how I'd behaved.

One day about a week later, when Mama heard the letter carrier make his morning delivery, she set the empty porridge pot in the sink and headed to the front door. She returned humming a lively hymn, waving two envelopes. Cleaning forgotten, she sat beside me at the kitchen table. "This one must be from Marja." *Toronto Free Hospital for Consumptives* was printed on the front of the envelope. She tore open the flap, and her face clouded as she scanned the brief letter. She handed it to Papa to read. "It's in English."

15 July 1914
Weston, Ontario

Dear Mrs. Maki,

I am a volunteer at the sanatorium. I am writing this letter on behalf of your sister, Marya. She is on complete bed rest and is not yet allowed time sitting up to write. She appears to now grasp this rule, especially after her knitting was confiscated.

Papa stopped reading and translating so that I could look up the definition of *confiscated* in the dictionary. Aunt Marja must have been livid to have her knitting taken away.

For the healing of her lungs to occur, it is essential that she remain lying down, doing absolutely nothing except eating and resting.

To me it sounded like royal treatment. But I couldn't imagine my aunt lying still all day. At the farm, the rare times she sat down were to milk cows, mend clothes, or peel vegetables.

Marya's fever and coughing have not worsened.
I encourage you to write to your sister, as letters from family will cheer her and help her to improve.

Yours truly,
Mrs. C. Appleby

"I'll start a letter to Auntie right now," I said, finding paper and pencil. Easier said than written. I chewed the end of my pencil, trying to decide what to say. Should I tell her about Gordon's plans? No, it should be lighthearted. Should I admit how I fell on my bottom learning to roller skate? "Mama, what should I write?"

She stared at Mrs. Appleby's letter as if trying to decipher the English words. "Marja would love to hear what Sanni is learning to do."

What did she mean? Sanni was a warm, cuddly sack; fresh milk went in one end and what came out the other was anything but fresh. The only skill she'd learned was to fill her lungs with air and howl. "What is she learning to do?"

"Haven't you noticed? She can focus on your face when you hold her. And she's discovered her fist and can bring it to her mouth to suck on it."

"Those things are worth writing about?" My mother was stranger than I thought.

"Marja would want to know *everything* about her daughter—including how long she sleeps at night."

Through the piece of hard sugar Papa held in his teeth, he slurped hot coffee from his saucer. "Weren't there two envelopes in the mail?"

Mama reached into her apron pocket, saying, "How could I forget?" She tore open the other envelope. As she pulled out the letter, a separate smaller piece of paper fluttered to the smooth, green linoleum and slid to my feet.

I stooped to retrieve it and recognized the Canadian Pacific Railway logo. My eyes grew large. It was a cheque made out to Emilia Maki for $162.00. I let out a joyful yelp. "We're rich!"

Papa's saucer clattered against the table as he set it down. "Let me see that." I handed over the cheque. His lower jaw fell. He whistled. He grabbed Mama and spun her around the room. "After this long I'd given up hope of a refund." But the CPR had kept its word and returned the cost of our *Empress of Ireland* tickets.

"Money is not king," said Mama. "As we say in the Old Country, 'You are rich if you have love.'" Trust my mother to teach a lesson.

"But now that we *have* extra money, will you buy me

47

a new bathing suit?" I asked. "And could I get my own pair of roller skates?"

"Nonsense, Saara," said Papa. "This money should go toward a down payment on a house."

Mama frowned. "We should save it for booking passage to Finland."

As much as I still wanted to meet my grandparents in Finland, I couldn't face boarding another steamship, not yet. The thought made a hard lump grow in my throat and my lungs squeeze with panic.

"There won't be any travelling if there's a war," said Papa.

Mama took me shopping the following day. We bought a new bathing suit—a proper neck-to-knee one in navy blue—and toiletries to send in a care package to Aunt Marja. Roller skates were out of the question. But Mama *did* splurge forty cents on a dozen Sunkist oranges—delicious.

"I know they're expensive," Mama confessed to Papa, "but we can redeem the wrappers for Rogers silverware."

By Sunday my parents were no closer to agreeing on what to do with the rest of the refund. We arrived early for the church service. Out of the corner of my eye I saw a flash of white on straw-coloured hair: Senja. If I was lucky during the week, I could avoid seeing her. But not on Sundays. She was wearing a gigantic hair bow made from six-inch-wide white ribbon. I couldn't stop staring.

"Gorgeous, isn't it, Saara?" she gloated.

More like grotesque or plain laughable.

"It's from Chapples—their most expensive ribbon,"

bragged Senja. "Edith and I took the streetcar by ourselves."

"Helena and I go to Fort William, too," I retorted. Taking the chance that she didn't know about my foot race prize, I said, "And I came back with a *gorgeous* bronze mirror." My, I sounded smug. I didn't like twisting the truth like that, but I took great delight in seeing Senja thrust her nose in the air and march away.

All through July, rumours of war filled the newspapers. It was getting so there was nothing else to read. I didn't want to write about war in my letters to Auntie. My big news for her was Sanni's first smile—which she had given to me.

By the twenty-eighth, Austria and Serbia were at war for real. The *Port Arthur Daily News* described Europe as being on the verge of the greatest war in history. What would that mean for us? We had our answer on July 31.

John dashed into the house, shouting, "*CANADA JOINS IN THE PREPARATIONS FOR BIG WAR!* That's today's headline." He gulped air and added, "Bully!" as if Canada were heading into a grand adventure. "Fred sold all his newspapers in no time."

"Papa, why do they call it a big war when there are only two countries fighting?" I asked, rocking Sanni, who was sucking her thumb.

"Because now there are more than two," replied Papa. "When Russia chose to back Serbia, Germany declared war on Russia, then on France. Russia and France are on the same side."

"That means they're allies, right?" asked John. "What side is Finland on?"

"Russia's," said Papa. "Finland is a grand duchy of Russia."

During the first week of August, Germany invaded Belgium, and Great Britain declared war on Germany. The "big war" had indeed come. When Richard next spotted me pushing the baby carriage, he shouted across the street, "Gordon enlisted! He's off to fight!"

For my family, life carried on the same after the war began. One mid-August day, at the exact moment I was teetering on a chair removing the used flypaper strip from the ceiling, the letter carrier delivered the afternoon mail. I speedily disposed of the long, sticky, housefly-coated paper in the garbage and hung a fresh yellowish-brown strip in its place. John fetched the stack of envelopes and handed it to Mama.

"Marja's handwriting!" said Mama.

She and I had both received a letter from Auntie. After getting Mrs. Appleby's weekly scribed notes, my heart fluttered at the sight of Auntie's script. Mama abandoned the raspberries she was preparing to can and retreated to the parlour with her envelope. In the privacy of the kitchen, I read my letter.

August 10, 1914

Dearest Saara,

I'm finally allowed to exert myself by writing. The doctors and nurses mean well, but this long month of lying in bed has been difficult to bear. There are no

books or magazines in Finnish, so I struggle to read the
English ones. My roommate, Josephine, from Toronto,
befriended me the moment I arrived. She does her best
to help me understand English with a great deal of hand
movements and charades.

I chuckled. It sounded like parlour games at a party.

Two other ladies share our room ~ Frances, from
Sudbury, and Rebecca, also from Toronto. Frances is
older, rather serious, a mother hen, while Rebecca is a
flighty (and dare I say rude) ~~young woman~~ *girl. The food*
is wholesome and plentiful ~ I'm growing positively fat.
Is the pie-faced woman in the bronze mirror truly me?
Thank you for the news of Sanni. Do give her an
extra kiss and cuddle from me. Josephine also has an
infant. Timmy's photograph dominates her bedside table.
If I understand her, he lives with her parents because
Josephine's husband has enlisted. Timmy's not allowed to
visit. We cry together, missing our babies, feeling sorry for
ourselves. Voi, voi ~ I shouldn't bore you. My fever is
gone and I don't cough as much. It won't be much longer
and I'll be on the train heading home.

I couldn't wait to see her again.

The day after Arvo left, I was driven to the central
part of Toronto where an X-ray was made ~ a picture
of my insides. My bones were white against a black
background, and the shadow of tuberculosis showed in
my left lung. It was most interesting, but I prefer my
image in our family portrait.

I pictured the family portrait in my mind. Uncle and Sanni were unchanged, but Aunt Marja was transformed into a skeleton bordered in black. A shiver crept along my back. I shook my head until my ears rang and the picture vanished.

The grumpy nurse (not Miss Hardy ~ she's an angel and I adore her) sneaked alongside my bed and startled me (that's why the ink blotted above). She said my "time up" was over. So I must end here and write to your mother tomorrow. I long to hold my little Sanni.

Love,

Aunt Marja

I wanted to read Mama's letter. She was still reading on the sofa, weeping into her handkerchief. Why was she crying? Auntie seemed fine to me. I ran upstairs to my bedroom and stowed my letter in the top dresser drawer.

Back in the kitchen, I grabbed the Old Dutch cleanser and began cleaning the icebox. If I finished the chore before Mama asked me to help her can the raspberries, I could leave for Helena's with a clear conscience. No girl in the history of iceboxes had ever scrubbed one so quickly and thoroughly.

Helena stood near the back door of their boarding house pegging diapers to the clothesline. Noticing me, she waved as though flagging down a train. What had gotten her fired up?

"Have you seen the newspaper?" she called.

I shook my head. "Is the war over?"

"I wish it were. My father hasn't enlisted yet, but he said a hundred thousand men have already signed up." She pulled me into the house and thrust the newspaper at me. "There's going to be a contest."

Something New for Babies— A Better Babies Contest

A Better Babies Contest is a scientific examination of children five years of age or under, for physical and mental development, and the awarding of prizes to babies making high scores.

"Let's enter our babies!" said Helena, rocking between heels and tiptoes.

I frowned. *Our* babies? Sanni wasn't *my* baby. Sure she'd lived with us for six weeks, and I enjoyed being around her as long as she wasn't fussing or wailing or needing to be changed. But she was still just my cousin. "You mean my cousin and your sister."

Helena shrugged. "Of course. Do you want to?"

"I guess so." If my best friend weren't so keen to enter, I'd have nothing to do with the contest. Sanni *had* become quite alert, though, with bright round eyes and lots of smiles for me. She'd begun "talking," an "a-a-w" sound with gurgles. That showed mental development, didn't it? And whenever I held her, she loved to press her feet hard against me, trying to stand.

Helena studied the contest notice. "It's based on good all-round development. We have ten days to get our babies smarter and stronger."

It was a relief to have a project to focus on as tensions grew in my house. Papa found piece-work jobs, but still no full-time work. Some days he found no work at all. I flinched when he slammed a rolled-up newspaper on the kitchen table.

"Prices for clothing and food here are rising because of the war in Europe," he said. "And tea is in short supply in Canada." I couldn't understand why that upset him when he drank coffee. It disturbed *me*, since I preferred tea.

According to Mama we were managing, but she was reluctant to spend any more of the refund money except in an emergency. As a seamstress, Mama sewed new clothes and altered old ones. The more sewing jobs Mama took on, the more I was needed to watch the baby and deliver garments. Papa had promised that I could help in the library in the Finnish Labour Temple, but whenever he asked, I had to look after Sanni and couldn't go.

One evening at supper, Mama told Papa, "I heard folks at the Co-Op say there should be more jobs coming available soon."

Papa looked doubtful.

"They said companies will need to replace the Port Arthur men who have signed up."

John startled us by jumping to his feet. He stood at attention, saluting. "Private Mäki reporting for duty, sir."

"Young man," said Papa sternly, yet winking in my direction, "report for duty at the woodpile by seven o'clock sharp."

I giggled. If Papa wanted to give John my chore of

refilling the woodbox, I was all for it. Mama handed Sanni and her glass bottle of milk to me. It served me right for gobbling my food. I'd have to feed and burp her while Mama ate. Sanni looked like a baby robin with her tiny mouth wide open waiting for nourishment. She frantically sucked the air as I shoved the big rubber nipple between her lips.

"I saw Richard Williams at the Co-Op yesterday," I said. "You know his brother, Gordon? Since he enlisted he gets paid a dollar a day and he has to live in the barracks, with an eight o'clock curfew at night. All he's done so far is guard the grain elevators."

"Do they think someone will steal the grain?" asked John. "Or blow up the buildings?"

"It's important to protect vital sites," said Papa. "I hear there are soldiers posted at the Kakabeka Falls power plant, and at wireless stations and dry docks."

I shrugged and said, "Gordon's tired of being made fun of and can't wait to go overseas."

I started a letter to Aunt Marja one evening the following week.

Port Arthur, Ont.
Aug. 21, 1914

Dear Auntie,

I'm entering Sanni in the Better Babies Contest on Tuesday and she's certain to win a prize. How do I know? Well, she's awfully bright, always catching your eye and giving you heaps of smiles.

Something wasn't quite right about that last sentence. When I read the words as if I were Auntie, it became clear as Lake Superior water. I crumpled the letter, tossed it into the wood stove, and pulled out a fresh sheet of paper. I rewrote the sentence:

Well, she's awfully bright, always catching my eye and giving me heaps of smiles. She babbles and is strong enough to hold her head up by herself. She is sure to impress the judges.

My ~~friend's~~ classmate's brother has enlisted. He's seventeen but told them he's eighteen. He's been sent to Valcartier in Quebec. He wrote home that whenever ladies boarded the train, they would wish him and anyone else in uniform good luck and a safe return. He's worried he won't get to Europe in time to fight. He says the war will be over by Christmas. You will be back well before Christmas and will beat the soldiers home. I miss you.

Love,
Saara

Right after I sealed the envelope, doubt began taking root in my heart. What if the soldiers beat Auntie home instead?

6

On the day of the Better Babies Contest, I picked up Sanni from her cradle and gasped. Across her scalp were scaly yellow patches.

"Mama, what's wrong with her head?"

Mama inspected Sanni. "You mean her skin? It's cradle cap. Nothing serious."

"Can you make it go away?"

"It must run its course, Saara. It could be weeks before it clears up."

"*Weeks?* She can't win the contest looking like a monster!"

"You could dress her in her prettiest bonnet and keep it on," suggested Mama.

I wasn't sure I should enter Sanni, after all. But I couldn't let Helena down.

At the Better Babies Contest, the waiting area was swarming with infants. They appeared to be in perfect health. It took every ounce of willpower for me to resist bolting. Instead Helena and I registered and found chairs together. Helena's hands trembled as if she were facing a school examination without having studied. She filled her lungs and exhaled, giving me a weak smile.

A tiny brusque woman called out Sanni's name and escorted us into the neighbouring room. She handed the registration form to the nurse and left, closing the door behind her.

"Good morning, miss," said the doctor, fixing his bespectacled eyes on my cousin. "Lay the baby right here." He pointed to the centre of a cloth-covered length of wood on the table. It looked like an upside-down bench.

The doctor removed Sanni's bonnet. My heart began to thump as I awaited his reaction. Nothing. He positioned Sanni at one end of the "bench" with her feet pressed against the vertical "leg." As he peered at the top of her head, I figured cradle cap would disqualify her. Instead he said, "Twenty-two and a half inches," which the nurse wrote on Sanni's form. Using a measuring tape, the doctor circled Sanni's head and called out, "Fifteen and one-quarter."

He was simply taking measurements. My shoulders relaxed and I could breathe normally.

By the end of the examination, every aspect of my cousin's body had been measured, including her weight: ten pounds, eleven ounces. They were supposed to test mental development, as well, but how?

After Mandi's turn, I found out how it was done with older babies. Helena's eyes shone with tears. The doctor had given Mandi instructions on handling objects, including dolls, but she didn't understand the English. When Helena began translating into Finnish, he stopped her. "The baby must follow the directions given in English." Mandi failed miserably. How unfair.

We left empty-handed. What a colossal waste of time. I could have spent the past ten days visiting Chief at the stables or practising my running.

Helena sniffled. I hooked my arm around her shoulders. "Who cares what Mandi scored," I told her. "We know she's intelligent."

"I'll never put us through that again."

"Anyway, there's no practical use for the trophy," I said.

"Not like your prize mirror. You do use it, don't you?" she asked, nudging me in the side and grinning.

"I gave it to my aunt. She must be using it because she told me she's getting plump."

"Does that mean she's getting well?" Helena leaned over, pushing hard on the carriage handle to climb the hill. Her cheeks were heat flushed.

"I wish I knew." The wicker creaked and the carriage wheels crunched on stones. A dog barked from behind a weathered board fence.

Approaching us on the sidewalk were Senja and Edith. There was no possibility of avoiding those snobby girls, but I intended to ignore them. As we passed them, we heard animated whispers.

Senja called after us, "Saara, did you know Edith's aunt in Timmins died of tuberculosis?"

I stopped in my tracks, my mouth gaping like a dead fish. "I … I …"

"I didn't know her well, but it was tragic," said Edith.

"She wasted away. Her five children were each adopted by a different family."

Helena tugged on my arm. "Don't pay attention to them," she said. "Knowing Senja, it's probably a lie, meant to upset you."

I shook my head to clear away their poison, and we kept walking. "Mama likes to say, 'Speak only the truth, even if it means only one word a day.'" I added, "If Senja abided by that proverb, she'd be mute."

"Saara—that's nasty," said Helena, but she giggled.

After we crossed Johnson Avenue, Helena took a breath as if to speak.

I raised my eyebrows. "What is it?"

"I shouldn't … but … I overheard my mother say that your aunt is in the 'clutch of consumption' and that tuberculosis is now the most common cause of death."

"Helena, don't you dare talk like that! You sound like Senja!"

"I'm sorry, I—"

"Aunt Marja will get better, I know it." I parked Sanni's carriage in front of the Star Livery. "I want to see Chief. Could you watch Sanni for a minute?"

"Go ahead. The shade will cool me down."

Elias was out driving, but Chief was in his box stall. He nickered when he saw me, pushing his sleek black head as far out of his stall as possible. I stroked his long nose with one hand and his silky neck with the other. He nuzzled my pockets, searching for a carrot stub. "Sorry, fella, I forgot your treat. Next time, I promise."

I'd never forget the thrilling ride he'd given us at New

Year's when my family sleighed to North Branch to visit Auntie and Uncle. The memory made my spirits sink. School would start in two weeks and I hadn't visited the farm all summer. I missed seeing Lila and helping with the animals and barn chores. Lila thought I was crazy to want to live there. She said she'd trade places with me in a heartbeat.

"Saara," called Helena from the livery's entrance. "We need to go."

"All right." My reflection stared at me from Chief's dark eye. I whispered, "You're the best chum. I forget your carrot, and you still love me. See you soon."

7

It was time to focus on school. I crammed my worrisome thoughts of Auntie deep inside me—tighter than preserved beef in a canning jar—next to memories of the *Empress* disaster. My Junior Fourth teacher, Miss Rodgers, was new to our school, and I took a liking to her the minute I entered the classroom. It wasn't her severe black skirt and uniform-like blouse, dark-framed glasses, and brown hair raked in a bun. It was her warm-hearted bubbling-brook laugh. A person who could make that sound was worth getting to know.

I steered Helena to a pair of desks on the opposite side of the classroom from Senja and Edith. Why invite problems from those troublemakers? As Miss Rodgers called us to attention, Richard slipped into the desk behind mine, whispering hello. My heart fluttered, not with happiness, but with dismay. It didn't matter whether he was sweet on me, as Helena thought, or he disliked me—his teasing was annoying just the same.

"Good morning, ladies and gentlemen," Miss Rodgers began. Her treating us as grown-ups made me smile.

After taking attendance, she led us in singing "God Save the King." Miss Rodgers read the Scripture verses from Ecclesiastes like poetry, her voice musical: "To every thing there is a season, and a time to every purpose under the heaven: A time to be born, and a time to die; a time to plant, and a time to pluck up that which is planted; A time to kill, and a time to heal … a time to mourn, and a time to dance … a time to keep silence, and a time to speak; A time to love, and a time to hate; a time of war, and a time of peace."

It was a time to heal for Auntie and a time for peace for the world.

"Each of you has a single sheet of foolscap in front of you. We will open our school year with writing an essay." The room erupted with groans, which she ignored. "Today, jot down your ideas. You will have a fortnight to complete your essay. I challenge each of you to consider your dreams and to set yourself goals for this year. What is Junior Fourth a time for, for you?"

She gazed around the room. "Identify your interests and strengths. Allow those aspects of your character to guide you in determining specific goals. Remember, young ladies, not to limit your options for the future." She returned to her desk at the front. "All of you, keep in mind that a dream is not a dream if you can accomplish it today. A dream is something you strive for."

I picked up my pencil and stared at the blank white space. Setting a few goals should be easy. But I couldn't think of any. All that swirled through my mind was the question I'd been plagued with since I survived the shipwreck: *What is the purpose of my life?* Why was I alive and not Lucy-Jane Blackwell? She had been so jolly and loving and good. Why had she died? Why had her parents, people of deep faith, lost their only child?

I glanced at my best friend sitting next to me. What would she write? As much as I loved Helena and would be loyal to her forever, I knew we were different. Apart from the threat of her father enlisting, her biggest worries seemed frivolous to me—her appearance, and when a boy would pay special attention to her and be her first beau. Me? I wanted to have fun. But I also longed to know the answer to that question, an answer that Mr. Blackwell was so confident existed. He thought nothing in life happened by chance.

Then what about Aunt Marja? Two years ago, we had spent an anxious time awaiting news of the fate of Auntie and her first husband, newlyweds immigrating to Canada aboard the *Titanic*. She had lost her husband; for what purpose was Auntie's life spared? Surely it was more than just to have Sanni and then die of tuberculosis?

These questions hurt my brain. In a way, I envied Gordon. This assignment would have been easy for him. His one goal was to get to France and battle for freedom: a noble purpose. All I could see for my life was sweeping floors and beating mats and washing dishes.

Miss Rodgers rose from behind her wooden desk. "That is all the time for today. When additional ideas come to you, record them for our next work session."

My paper contained the single word "purpose." It was underlined and circled several times. I had pressed so hard that my pencil tip tore through, marking my desk. I couldn't remember ever feeling so relieved to start arithmetic.

At dismissal, Miss Rodgers asked me to stay behind. "I noticed your intense concentration this morning ..." I beamed, pleased at her praising my efforts on the first day. "... however, I also saw a lack of writing for your essay preparation." My smile vanished as I studied the scuffed tips of my boots. "Have you any ideas, Saara?"

"Well, I've been thinking ..."

"There was a veritable wrestling match in your head, I think. Is something troubling you?"

Her genuine concern melted my intentions of making a positive first impression. In a shaky voice, I told my story. She listened without interrupting.

"The accident on the *Empress* was ghastly ... horrid. I want to forget it. My family's had our share of tragedy. It's time for better things. But now my aunt has tuberculosis and is in the sanatorium in Toronto." I stumbled through explaining the questions the essay topic raised for me.

"Oh, Saara. I moved here from Toronto a week ago. I was ignorant of your trauma." Her eyes were full of warmth. "Those are overwhelming events and thoughts for any age, but especially for twelve."

"It's okay, Miss Rodgers," I said, sucking in a big breath. "I can do the assignment."

She nodded. "I trust you can, my dear. Should you have the need to discuss your ideas, you are always welcome to talk with me."

"Thank you, Miss Rodgers." As I turned to go, she touched my shoulder.

"Saara, the Toronto sanatorium is one of the best in the world."

My eyes instantly flooded.

That night, it wasn't only Sanni who woke me, but my usual *Empress* nightmare, too.

CHAPTER

8

The school nurse visited our classroom on Friday. Her white uniform's long skirt rustled as she moved from desk to desk, inspecting our fingernails and teeth. She clucked her disapproval several times. "I thought by your age there would be no need to teach you basic hygiene. Very well. Watch as I demonstrate correct fingernail care and tooth brushing."

I leaned back and whispered, "Pay attention, Richard." He jerked my right braid. "You, too, farmer girl."

What was wrong with liking farm life? Besides, it was there Auntie had taught me to thoroughly clean my hands so that I wouldn't contaminate the cows' milk.

The nurse led us in a nose-blowing drill. "Always carry a handkerchief. To avoid catarrhal conditions, you must maintain clean nasal passages." Once the first giggle escaped from a student, the whole class laughed. The boys looked ridiculous holding the starched white handkerchiefs to their noses. They were accustomed to holding a finger against one nostril and letting fly from the other—usually outdoors.

"Furthermore," said the nurse, "you must refrain from spitting and remember to smother your cough, in case you are infected with tuberculosis. It's become so rampant that I've been requested to examine each student for signs of the disease."

When Dr. Koljonen had examined me after Auntie was tested, I was clear. But Auntie hadn't smothered her cough until he had given her a mask. So my legs quivered as I stepped forward to be first in line. The nurse listened through her stethoscope to my breathing and coughing. After a few moments she pronounced me healthy.

When the nurse finished her examinations, she announced, "Commencing next week, for six weeks on Tuesdays after school I will be conducting classes to teach girls who have infant siblings how to care for them. The program is based on the popular 'Little Mothers' Classes' developed by a school nurse in Toronto. Girls who do not have an infant sibling may participate if they obtain permission to borrow a baby for the class."

I wasn't surprised when Helena's eyes lit up or when she asked whether I'd attend with her.

"Okay," I replied, with no enthusiasm. I got enough of baby care at home.

Richard followed us outside at dismissal, chuckling. "The little mothers go to school." He hummed a note, then sang, "Saa-ra has a lit-tle babe, lit-tle babe, lit-tle babe; Saa-ra has a lit-tle babe, its dress is white as snow—"

"Stop, Richard," I commanded, "or we'll borrow a colicky baby and sign you up for the class."

68

His grin widened. "It fol-lowed her to school one day, school one day ..."

I plugged my ears with my fingers and marched ahead. Helena thought Richard's antics were hilarious. At his house, Richard turned toward the front steps. I unblocked my ears. He was still singing. "... ev'ry-where that Saa-ra went, that babe was sure to go."

After school on Tuesday, Helena rushed us home to collect the babies and go back. The nurse began the first class for "little mothers" by lecturing on the danger of tuberculosis. She insisted that milk be pasteurized for babies fed cow's milk. Since we'd been doing exactly that for Sanni, I smugly and correctly answered her questions as to how high and how long to heat milk.

There was an oval wash basin set up on a table at the front of the classroom. The nurse picked up Doris's baby brother, saying, "I need to borrow him for the demonstration." He wailed. I expected her to pass him right back to Doris, but instead she gave us a lesson on settling fussy children. She rocked him and cooed. She jiggled him as she walked, until the baby stopped crying. She removed his long dress, booties, and stockings, leaving the diaper on. Without using water, the nurse taught us the proper technique for bathing an infant.

Everyone practised—without water, as well, but with a bar of soap and with the babies fully clothed. It's a wonder no one dropped her baby with the amount of tittering over how foolish we looked. Sanni grabbed the soap and squealed with happiness. She jammed the corner of it in her mouth before I could retrieve it.

The nurse frowned. "Babies will reach for anything—watch them carefully."

I blushed and glared at Sanni. She smiled, drooling a bubble. The class couldn't end too soon.

I avoided Miss Rodgers's essay for as long as I could, pretending I had all year to write it. Then it was due in two days. I wished I could simply say, "My goal is to have fun. My strength is memorizing recitations. I dream of becoming an actress." While the statements were truthful, they weren't sufficient for a whole essay. I forced myself to think hard, and again the question of purpose took over. What if the only purpose in *my* life being spared had already passed, when I saved *John's* life? Was that it for me? Or was there more? Sighing, I figured I wouldn't know the answer until I became an adult, and an old one at that. There was no point in trying to guess. What a stupid assignment!

I slammed my pencil down on the kitchen table. Perhaps drinking a cup of tea would help me sort through my turmoil. I stoked the fire in the wood stove and set the kettle of water to heat.

Goals. Dreams. I stamped my foot like an impatient horse. I used to dream of being a princess, until I learned you had to be born one or marry a prince. Then I dreamed of money—it was a constant struggle for our family to pay the rent and feed and clothe us. To always have enough money to buy what we needed would be incredible. I used to dream of travelling to Finland. Was that still my dream? Yes. I had been thwarted by the *Empress* and now the war, but I longed to visit the place my family came from.

Miss Rodgers didn't want girls to limit their options for the future. She likely thought we should go further in our schooling. I huffed and crossed my arms. I hadn't thought of doing that. What I most wanted was to have my own farm. The more that motorized vehicles took over Port Arthur streets, the more I wanted to move to the country. But how could that ever work out? The offer of cheap farmland wasn't for women. One solution would be if Uncle Arvo sold part of his farm to me. But how would I earn enough money? How old would I need to be?

I sorely missed having time there as I'd had last summer. I remembered the day Uncle and I were cleaning the sweat-stained, mud-caked harnesses. "Use lots of elbow grease, Saara," he said. So I pressed harder to scrub the dirty leather. "When Ace and Copper were pulling the wagon uphill, did you notice how Ace is starting to show his age?"

"He was breathing harder and slowing Copper down."

"He'll need to be replaced in a year or two and I'm determined to buy a Canadian horse."

"Aren't all the workhorses Canadian?"

He laughed. "I meant the breed, not where they're born. A Quebec teamster at the lumber camp last winter boasted about the Canadian breed—a superior farm horse, he said. Compact but strong. He claimed one Canadian horse hauled a skid of logs loaded higher than what the biggest draft horse could pull."

Perhaps Uncle could get a pregnant mare and he (we!) could raise and train the foal. That idea set my heart romping. My goal could be spending time at the Star Livery learning more about horse care from Elias. Miss Rodgers hadn't said the goal must be accomplished in the classroom, had she? Hurrah! A real goal to write about.

The kettle boiled over; water sputtered onto the stove lids. *Hiss.* Steam billowed. I quickly brewed tea and returned to my writing assignment.

Mama received a weekly letter from Auntie, but I had to wait until October for my next one.

September 27, 1914

Dearest Saara,
  Hello from prison.

Prison? What an odd choice of word.

Life here isn't that bad, but at times I feel trapped and I don't know how long the judge (Dr. Dobbie) will make me stay. One thing is bad ~ the coffee. It has a strange taste. I crave good strong Finnish boiled coffee. I miss the sauna, too. At least I've progressed from bed baths to tub baths (bed baths were awful as I never felt clean). There's one more horrible thing. My favourite nurse, Miss Hardy, has answered the call for Field Nurses for the war and will be sailing to England on October 1. She is the one nurse who makes this place bearable. I'll miss her terribly. She promised to write to us, but I doubt she'll have time or energy.

Here's a riddle for you. I was permitted outside for a walk yesterday, but I couldn't leave my bed. How could that be accomplished? Do you give up?

I mulled over the riddle but remained baffled.

I felt like a baby in a carriage. The nurse helped me transfer into a wicker bed on wheels. Mrs. Appleby wheeled me out into the glorious sunshine. She took me across the property to see the Queen Mary Hospital for Tuberculous Children. It has grand stone pillars at the front. The patients' schoolroom has no desks ~ it's the balcony! The students must remain in their beds. Can you imagine if they tipped their ink bottles? The housekeeper would be furious!

What a nasty mess that would be!

Outside I also saw the most unusual accommodation for male patients ~ ten old horse-drawn streetcars. One or two men live in each streetcar. A few of them have cheery garden plots out front.

Josephine humours me with jokes. It takes so long for her to explain them to me with hand motions that sometimes she gives up and I feel awful. Once I laughed too early, wanting to make it easier for her, but she knew I didn't understand. I wish my English were better.

I'm not allowed to clear my throat without a handkerchief to my mouth. And I must collect my sputum (yes, your auntie must SPIT like a man into a container).

Try as I might, I could not picture my aunt aiming for a spittoon.

If I could sell what I cough up, I'd be rich. I reread that sentence and realized it sounds crass. I'm sorry, Saara, but living in a sanatorium makes us view bodily functions in a whole different way. We'd go stir-crazy if we couldn't poke fun at the routines here.

You asked how long it will take for me to get well. Be assured that I intend to be cured as fast as is humanly possible and be home for Christmas dinner. Give my sweet little girl a hug and smother her with kisses from me.

Love,
Aunt Marja

Not home until Christmas? She'd already been gone for three months, and I'd have to wait another three.

At school the next day, Richard was bursting with news. "If you want to see history in the making, look here," he said, handing Miss Rodgers a newspaper clipping. Curious, Helena and I stood on either side of her to read the advertisement.

"I'm going on Saturday to watch the war reel," said Richard. "I want to see what my brother's in for. We got a letter from Gordon yesterday. He wrote it the day before he sailed to England on the *Franconia*."

I wondered whether Gordon was on the same ship as Auntie's favourite nurse.

Miss Rodgers asked, "Did your brother say how soon he will be in France?"

"No. He expects to spend a while training in England.
But he won't be happy until he's in the trenches at the
front line."

"That sounds all too familiar." She looked unusually
serious. "My brother joined the forces, as well—in
September, the very day he turned eighteen."

After school, Helena and I and the babies attended
the fourth Little Mothers' Class. The nurse had already
instructed us on common illnesses and feeding of infants.
In each class she warned of the danger of tuberculosis
and stressed the need to pasteurize cow's milk. When
she said, "Infants need to spend plenty of time in the
fresh air and sunshine," I grinned. We Finns had been
following that healthy practice for ages.

First thing Monday morning, Miss Rodgers announced that our class would mount a spring drama production. Over the summer she'd written a play called *Aedgiva's Quest*. I had never had a teacher with such ambition. We would give two performances, on the last Friday and Saturday of March.

"The play is set in medieval times," she said, the heels of her boots striking the floor as she marched between our desks. "Young Princess Aedgiva's quest is to free her imprisoned brother Rupert." Miss Rodgers stopped mid-row, staring out the window. Whispers trickled around the room. She cleared her throat and continued, . "Auditions for the lead roles will take place on January 15. I will, however, base my decisions in part on your Christmas concert performances." She sounded her pitch pipe to begin our opening exercises with "God Save the King."

My mouth sang the words, but my thoughts were glued to *Aedgiva's Quest*. Could the play be the answer to *my* quest? Was my purpose to become a famous actress, after all? The idea grew more appealing. I longed to repeat my grand recitation from last year's Christmas concert—and wipe out the memory of my grand flop from the Empire Day ceremonies last May. How juvenile of me to have bolted from the school when I forgot my lines. I needed to work extra hard on my memorization. Papa would be so proud of me if I won the lead role.

Miss Rodgers returned our essays at dismissal. She'd given me a high mark. She must have liked my goals. I slowly descended the stairs, absorbing her comments: *This grade reflects the technical quality of your writing. With that, I found little to fault. But as far as the depth of the content is concerned, I had expected more.* Did she think further schooling was the *only* worthwhile goal? I stuffed the essay inside my Junior Fourth reader. I had a new goal to focus on: to be cast as Aedgiva!

Later the next week, both Mama and I got letters from Auntie. I tore open mine:

October 17, 1914

Dearest Saara,

Thank you for writing. Your letter was the bright spot of my week. My little Sanni is laughing ~ imagine that! Oh, how I'd love to hold her and hear her laugh.

What a busy time you're having at school already. I'm pleased that you find Miss Rodgers so agreeable.

You asked what is new here. Well, in the beginning I had to stay in bed day and night. I memorized the ceiling pattern and the nicks on the iron railing at the

*foot of my bed. Josephine was not allowed time up out
of bed until after she'd been here six months. Thank
heavens for me it began after three months. At first all
the nurses let me do was sit up in bed for a few minutes
a day. Gradually my time up grew longer until I was
allowed to get out of bed and walk in the corridors.
Now that I'm allowed to exercise, I walk outside each
day no matter how wet or cool the weather. This land
used to be the Buttonwood Farm. I'm enclosing a map
I sketched of the grounds so you can picture where I am.
My room is on the second storey of the Main Medical
Building (I wish I had a view of the Humber River).
I've never been inside the King Edward Building. It's
for paying patients. The Connaught Home was opened
on May 29. It's hard to imagine any celebration on the
same day as the Empress disaster.*

A chill gave me shivers from the inside out. I hated
being reminded of the *Empress*.

*The Assembly Hall is under construction (very noisy). It
will be wonderful for patients to attend concerts there,
but I intend to be long gone by the time it's completed
next year. Glenwyld is the home of the Medical Director,
Dr. Dobbie, and his wife. He's a giant of a man, and
most kind. You must think I've become a busybody. Mrs.
Appleby loves to chatter and each outing in my rolling
bed was a narrated tour. She repeated herself so often I
think I've got it straight.*

*Next to the children's home stands an ancient oak
tree ~ the largest tree I've ever seen. Josephine says it's*

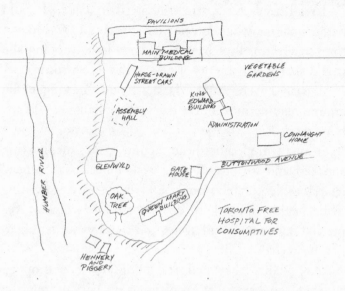

a lovely shady spot for picnics and "croquet" (she wrote down the word for me ~ is it a game?). I missed the summer activities lying in bed.

My favourite place to rest when I'm out for exercise is on the edge of the escarpment overlooking the river. The view is beautiful, but better still (don't laugh) is the smell from the hennery and piggery ~ it reminds me of the homestead. Some days I can't stay long because I miss home so terribly.

I'm sending my kisses for Sanni. Will you please deliver them? For me, knowing you are keeping your promise to help watch my baby is a great comfort being this far away.

> Love,
> Aunt Marja

I read her letter again, studying her sketch. I could better imagine what Auntie's day-to-day life was like at the sanatorium. I let Mama read my letter, hoping she would share the contents of hers with me. She didn't.

"I wish I were Aunt Marja," I said, "getting to lie around reading most of the day and not having to do any housework."

Mama whipped her head around to face me, looking shocked and furious. "Never wish for such an illness! Marja is desperately lonely and would give anything to be healthy enough to do housework." Mama's eyes pierced my own. "You haven't said that in your letters to her, have you?"

"No, Mama," I replied, trembling. My gaze dropped to Sanni on her quilt. From lying on her tummy, she rolled onto her back and waved her arms.

"Ma," said Sanni. I sat back, startled. Was she saying "Mama"? I hadn't heard her say a word before.

Mama didn't appear to notice. She was deep in thought, as if choosing her words with extreme care. "Marja needs willpower strong enough to take her through stone to win this battle."

What did she mean? I was afraid to ask. Auntie sounded fine to me—confident and in good spirits. My mother always fretted too much.

Her comment worried me, though. I decided against telling Auntie about Sanni's new word.

November brought the first snowfall, making the lane beside our house slippery on Friday after school.

"Halt! Who goes there?" shouted John—"Private Mäki"—as he jabbed his stick rifle at me.

I startled, fumbling my textbooks and scribblers. One book fell. I retrieved it from the thin white blanket of snow. Another armed "soldier"—Fred—appeared around the corner of our porch.

"You two must have run all the way to beat me home."

"State your name and rank," ordered Fred, poking my school books with the tip of his "rifle." The soldiers barred my way by crossing their weapons.

Both boys wore enamel wash basins as helmets. It was difficult to stifle my laughter when the basins slipped off and clattered onto the steps. The sooner I played along with their war game, the sooner I'd get inside.

"Saara Mäki, Chief Bottlewasher."

"Entry granted." Fred and John hoisted their pretend rifles onto their shoulders and marched away on drill practice.

Indoors, it was quiet except for Mama's soft snoring from the parlour. She must have fallen asleep on the sofa after settling Sanni for her nap. These days, my cousin fussed and drooled continually and her nose streamed snot that turned crusty. Disgusting. I padded into the kitchen to find something to eat.

From upstairs came the sound of Sanni snuffling. I sliced a chunk of rye bread and sank my teeth into the chewy crust. Sanni cried. As soon as I finished eating, I would go to her. But her cry rapidly shifted into a wail. Mama rushed past me to the stairs without saying hello, as if she were wearing leather blinkers like a horse.

I wandered into the parlour, where an opened letter lay on the floor. It was from Aunt Marja to Mama. My conscience twinged, telling me I shouldn't read it, but I ignored the warning.

October 26, 1914

Dearest Emilia,

I wrote as cheery a letter as I could muster to our Saara. Please forgive me, but if I don't unburden the depths of my heart to someone it will break into a thousand pieces. I cannot tell Arvo. You are the one person to whom I can reveal the truth.

The stop signal from my conscience grew urgent. Curiosity tempted me to keep going.

I've heard of patients whose marriages have fallen apart because of their long stay in the sanatorium. It frightens me to the core. I cannot bear the thought of losing Arvo. Promise you'll burn these pages the instant you have read them so that no other human eyes will see my painful words. I want no record of this bitter time.

My conscience blared like a siren and flashed lights. I knew I ought to stop reading, but I couldn't bring myself to put the letter down.

As you know, I've been allowed time up to exercise. What I didn't realize ~ I am so stupid! ~ is that the doctor meant slow walking. I'd become so restless lying in bed and plump beyond belief. You wouldn't recognize me.

I was overjoyed to spend time outdoors and was practically running. It was too much exertion, and now I must pay the price. I'm confined to bed again with absolutely NO time up (I'm writing this lying down ~ Josephine is my sentry, to warn me if a nurse approaches ~ I'm not supposed to be writing but I must disobey to survive). The fever has struck again and I'm coughing as before. This disease is <u>horrible</u>. The nurses warned me if any symptoms returned I would be promptly sent to bed. How could I feel perfectly well and overnight feel wretched? I'm desperate to improve so I can return home before Christmas. But now it seems impossible, though I pray to God every waking moment.

Impossible? But Aunt Marja had told me all along that she'd be home for Christmas. What was going on? My stomach pitched and my legs jellied. I could no longer trust them to hold me upright, so I sank onto the sofa.

It's now October 27. Knowing how despondent I feel as an adult, I can't imagine what it must be like for the children here with tuberculosis. They are uprooted from their families and no matter how caring the nurses, they could never replace the children's devoted mothers in giving them the love they need to thrive.

Nothing cheers me but letters from family. The food is of good quality, lots of fresh eggs and meat, but tasteless to me. I never noticed the dropping temperature while I was able to walk outdoors. The windows are always kept open as the fresh air is good for our lungs. Now that I'm trapped in bed I wear every stitch of clothing to keep warm ~ and it's not yet November. How will I last when winter arrives? Dr. Dobbie insists we spend part of the day on the balcony swathed in blankets "taking the cure." The sunlight helps our lungs. It's better than my "jail cell," but no matter how tightly the nurse wraps me, I shiver.

Voi, voi. Emilia, I try to keep my spirits up, but life is tedious. The nurses record every detail of my personal health, from how long I sleep, to how much I cough, to the colour of my sputum. There's no end to the coughing in this place, especially at night ~ and disgusting sounds of throat clearing and spitting. I'm used to it now, but there were times my stomach would get the heaves and I'd lose my supper.

I can't find the words to express how grateful I am to you for taking Sanni into your home. Thank you, too, for the care packages ~ you have sacrificed so much for me.

Another day has passed and the horrors increase. Last night, young Rebecca made a ghastly choking noise. Josephine got a nurse. Rebecca was hemorrhaging from the lungs. The staff whisked her away. Tragically, she bled too much and died. I could not stop shaking for ages after hearing the news. While she was not my favourite person, I had no wish for her to suffer so. Today I learned she'd been a patient here for more than a year. Dear Frances is becoming more listless and has a serious infection in her sinuses. The rumour is she has miliary tuberculosis ~ the bacteria spreading through her bloodstream ~ always fatal. Honestly, I fear she, too, will succumb. Voi, voi. Emilia, how long must I be away? What will become of me? My heart aches for home.

With much love and trepidation,
Marja

If a boulder had landed on my head, I couldn't have been more stunned. Auntie had hidden so much from me, protecting me from the truth. Tears sprang from my eyes. Hearing Mama on the stairs, I panicked. I couldn't let her know I'd seen the letter. I placed it on the floor and slipped outside, careful not to bang the porch door.

Auntie's letter flooded me with horrid emotions and troubling images. I'd had no idea she was so ill. I dashed up the Bay Street hill to my lookout spot. It was too snowy for me to sit on my rock. Instead I hugged a tree trunk, welcoming something solid to cling to. The letter's honesty forced me to face the real Saara. I'd promised Auntie I would help care for Sanni, to ease my mother's burden. But I did as little as possible, looking for opportunities to get out of caring for her. I resented my cousin for making me miss out on fun. I often pretended not to hear Sanni waking from her nap so Mama would have to deal with her. How selfish.

Burning with shame, I said aloud, "I'm sorry, Auntie … and Mama …" I swallowed the colossal lump in my throat. "… and Sanni." I had to make things right. What could I do to help the time pass more quickly for my aunt? How could I be most helpful to Mama? With a stroke of insight, I knew the answers to both questions. I sprinted down the hill into the biting wind off the lake. It made my eyes water. I was thankful—it would disguise my crying. I had to take great care never to reveal my knowledge of Auntie's letter.

In the kitchen, Mama bounced a cranky baby on one hip while trying to fry meatballs.

I took Sanni and cuddled her, kissing her downy head. I knew exactly how to help Mama. "Could we move Sanni's cradle into my bedroom for tonight? I *promise* I'll look after her so you can sleep."

"Thank you, Saara. I am so exhausted, it's worth a try."

The first time I woke that night wasn't due to Sanni. In a panic, I felt I couldn't breathe. My dream of Auntie underwater faded away; I remembered where she was. I prayed she hadn't taken a turn for the worse. It took ages to relax and return to sleep.

Much to my relief, I sprang out of bed at the first whimper from inside the cradle. How odd to be awake in the middle of the night caring for Sanni. At one point she burped so loudly I expected the upstairs windows to rattle. I was proud to be able to rock her back to sleep in a still and slumbering household.

When I carried Sanni downstairs in the morning, Mama was straining runny porridge through the sieve. She beamed at me. "I never heard a peep from Sanni. Sleeping that long felt so refreshing." She stretched her arms. "It's time we start feeding Sanni warm cereal and wean her off milk during the night."

Papa stopped eating his porridge and looked my way. "You are definitely growing up, Saara-*kulta*." Saara-gold. I grinned.

10

On John's ninth birthday, Mama asked me to buy him a treat of Cocoa Dips from the confectionery. The snow had melted, so I offered to take Sanni along in her carriage. At the corner, Fred bellowed, *"CANADIAN TROOPS INSPECTED BY KING AND QUEEN."* I waved to him as he gulped air and continued, *"BITTER WEATHER AT FRONT: MEN FROZEN TO DEATH AMONG GERMAN TROOPS."*

On our way home I stopped to pat Chief. He stood facing uphill, hitched to a livery wagon outside the barber shop. I couldn't reach Chief's head and keep one hand on the baby carriage handle, so I braked the rear carriage wheels with stones.

A motor roared in the distance, much louder than an automobile's. It was one of those new contraptions—a motorcycle—heading our way. When the rider revved the motor, Chief flicked back his ears, snorted, and shied. A tingle shot up my backbone. Sanni joined the ruckus with her crying. I took hold of Chief's bridle and crooned, "Steady now, whoa, boy." He trembled with fear.

My heart pounded. Sanni wailed and kicked, shaking her carriage.

When the motorcycle passed the wagon, the man turned and laughed at the terrified horse. He accelerated. The back wheel sprayed gravel at Chief. He screamed and reared. I lost my grip. If I didn't calm him, he might bolt.

As I reached for Chief's bridle again, a movement caught my eye—Sanni's carriage was rolling backwards! Catch Sanni or hold Chief? What should I do? Fighting my urge to aid Chief, I leaped to grab the carriage.

Sanni was safe, but the motorcycle backfired going up the hill and spooked Chief. He bolted. "Chief, stop!" I cried.

"What's going on?" It was Elias.

"A motorcycle! You have to stop Chief!" I blurted.

"Idiot rider!" yelled Elias as he ran after Chief.

I watched in horror. Another horse and buggy entered the intersection where Chief and the careering wagon were headed. I shut my eyes. My insides roiled, stomach threatening to empty. I shook like poplar leaves in a gale and had to brace myself against the baby carriage handle.

I heard no crash, so I opened my eyes. Chief and the wagon had narrowly missed the buggy. He ran out of steam on the grade, allowing Elias to catch him. Slowly my pulse returned to normal. Chief was limping, but it didn't look serious.

Sanni bawled. What if I hadn't stopped her carriage from rolling? It would have toppled into the street, dumping Sanni out and … My throat tightened. I would have been devastated. Despite knowing I'd done the right thing in protecting Sanni, I was horrified that I'd had to think about choosing my cousin over a horse. It should have been automatic.

Twilight was fading to night. It had to be after five o'clock. Mama would be wondering what was taking us so long. My legs shaky, I pushed Sanni's carriage uphill. I waved to Elias as he led Chief past, but he was too preoccupied with the horse's foreleg to notice.

I threw myself wholeheartedly into helping Mama take care of Sanni. When it got to be a habit, it was time to follow through on my idea of making the stay at the sanatorium more enjoyable for Auntie. With pencil in hand, I spent an entire evening crafting the letter. In the morning I took care to address the envelope properly and mailed it. I had to wait three long weeks before I received a letter back from Auntie.

November 29, 1914

Dearest Saara,

How can I ever thank you? Today I had the pleasure of a visit from your friends, the Blackwells ~ my first visitors in five months. How thoughtful of you to write to them about my situation. They are such kind and caring people to take time on their Sunday to come here. They even located a Finnish domestic who could be released from her housekeeping duties to come along to translate for us. She lent me three Finnish books. While I appreciate the Finnish newspapers your mother sends, at last I have stories to get lost in.

A warmth spread through me as I saw how my one letter to the Blackwells had made a difference.

At bedtime the other night, a nurse asked, "Would you like a pig in bed with you?" My English has improved a little, but I thought I'd heard her wrong. I replied, "A pig?" and pushed my nose up with my finger and snuffled. Josephine exploded with laughter while I remained confused. The nurse brought a crockery "pig" filled with hot water to warm my bed. I was grateful but so embarrassed.

Having to return to bed rest has made the time pass more slowly than a glacier retreating. I hope to have time up again soon. Meanwhile, my restlessness increases and my tolerance for the tedious routine diminishes. But why complain about the inevitable? Success will not come unless I do what is necessary to heal my body. Josephine is living proof that following doctor's orders makes a difference. Besides being allowed to exercise, she is helping with the housekeeping. There's no pay, of course. When my turn comes, I hope the authorities will permit me to labour in the hennery or piggery. There I can build my stamina for returning to farm chores.

A third of the patients at this hospital are women, and many are immigrants. Among us are different religions and backgrounds, but we all have tuberculosis and we all yearn for the day when we're sent home.

Love,

Aunt Marja

Knowing what she'd written to Mama, I wondered how much worse it truly was for Auntie. What was I *not* being told in her letters to me?

I found my parents in the parlour when I arrived home from delivering a customer's altered skirt on Monday. Sanni squealed, spitting out the grey rubber rattle she was gumming, and waved to me from beside Mama on the sofa. Her welcome felt better than winning a spelling bee. I sat cross-legged on the floor and pulled her down onto my lap.

Papa was reading a Finnish newspaper and Mama was knitting a brownish-green scarf. Yesterday she'd finished a pair of warm blue socks for Auntie, so I asked, "Is that for Aunt Marja, too?"

She snorted. "You think I'd use this dreary khaki colour for her? This is a comfort for a soldier overseas." I was amazed at how she could knit and look at me at the same time. "The church Ladies' Aid Society is meeting here Thursday evening, so you'll need to look after Sanni."

"Of course, Mama. Is it the Society or your Sewing Circle that's making the scarves?"

"The Society. We're providing mittens, as well." Mama shook her head. "I fear the Sewing Circle is no longer my place. There's less sewing and more fundraising for the socialist local. It should be called a 'Study Circle.'" The focus is political, with the discussion centred on socialism."

Study. I hadn't started studying my Christmas concert recitation. How could I have forgotten? I'd practise right after supper.

Mama continued, "I agree with the emphasis on women's education and their right to work." Papa lowered the newspaper to listen. "But the last speaker was an avid socialist and an agitator against anything religious. She openly opposed the church and said marriage didn't need the blessing of an agent of heaven."

Mama sounded quite agitated herself. With her faith in God and commitment to our church, I could see her being upset. Sanni grabbed her rubber rattle and shoved the biting ring into her mouth.

"It sounds to me as if you've already decided to quit," said Papa.

The Big Finn Hall was run by the socialist local. Mama had refused to let me see some plays with anti-church themes, but I hoped she wouldn't ban me from going altogether or stop me from helping in the library.

Sanni laughed at the rustle of the newspaper when Papa turned the page. He said, "The war's getting closer to home. Listen to this: *PORT ARTHUR TO MAKE SHELLS AND OTHER MUNITIONS OF WAR FOR BRITISH GOVERNMENT*. Hmm ..." His eyes scanned the page. "It says here they're thinking of building submarines at Western Dry Dock. If so, they'll be hiring."

"Working on munitions could be dangerous," said Mama, knitting her brow as well as the scarf.

"But it would pay well and we need to eat."

As if Sanni could understand Papa's words, she howled for her supper. I let her suck on my upturned baby finger while we waited for Mama to mash a boiled potato.

"Ouch." Something scraped my finger. I peeked into Sanni's mouth and my eyes widened. "Mama, look! She's got her first tooth."

"It's uncanny how similar she is to you as a baby," said Mama, smiling. "You two could be sisters." At that moment I realized how bound I was to my cousin. I'd already started to think of her as my sister.

I practised my recitation for the Christmas concert while peeling potatoes, washing dirty pots, stocking the woodbox, and even bathing Sanni and changing her diapers. Staring into her huge blue eyes, I perfected my delivery. At least I'd try to. It was hard to be serious when presenting to a smiling, drooling half-year-old who's attempting to stuff her entire fist into her mouth.

By December 18, the day of the concert, I could recite the poem backwards. There was no need for Miss Rodgers to remind me she was judging our performances. My confidence swelled when I saw her glowing face as I recited my piece.

The applause was thunderous. Yet it was equally exuberant after Doris's recitation and *also* after Senja's. "Drat," I said under my breath. Competition for the part of Aedgiva would be fierce. The audition was in four weeks. I wished Miss Rodgers would hand out the scripts already, so I could prepare over the Christmas break. But when I asked, she was adamant. "Not until the first day of school in January."

CHAPTER

11

Mama insisted we clean the house from bedrooms to basement during the week before Christmas. We also baked cookies, cake, and *pulla*. Uncle Arvo had a winter job at a lumber camp, and he sent word that he would spend Christmas at the homestead. He wanted to relieve Mr. Koski of caring for the livestock. He would come for New Year's Eve.

I kept hoping all week that Auntie would appear— but there wasn't even a letter from her.

On Christmas Eve, my family went to Helena's house for a sauna and a feast. Would Joulupukki come, too, with his sack of gifts? The tables were laden with ham, carrots, beet salad, turnip loaf, and, of course, potatoes. What was Auntie eating in the sanatorium? Her baby's first taste of turnip ended up spat on the floor. Helena and I stuffed ourselves and quietly groaned when Mrs. Pekkonen brought out dessert. She served rice pudding with an almond hidden inside.

I poked my spoon through my serving, hoping to find

the nut. I felt the unmistakable hard lump. "I got the almond!"

"Good fortune will come your way, Saara," said Mr. Pekkonen.

"I wish Aunt Marja could have the almond instead." Around the table, smiling faces turned grim and heads nodded.

"Mr. Pekkonen, is it time to light the candles?" asked John.

"It's time." Helena's father pushed back from the table. Papa helped him light the tiny candles fastened to the Christmas tree's branches. Each one added brilliance to the tree until it shone like the sun. As soon as the last candle was lit, Mr. Pekkonen read the Christmas gospel. Afterward we began singing one of Martin Luther's hymns:

> *From Heaven above to earth I come*
> *To bear good news to every home …*

Every home in the British Empire would welcome good news that the war was over, especially with the reports of heavy losses for Britain. Our home would welcome good news about Auntie. Tears sprang to my eyes as I thought of her not being home as we had hoped for and expected. She must be incredibly sad, so far away from us.

> *To you, this night, is born a Child*
> *Of Mary, chosen mother mild;*
> *This tender Child of lowly birth,*
> *Shall be the joy of all your earth.*

On the floor, away from the blazing evergreen, sat Mandi holding Sanni's hand. Their eyes sparkled in the candlelight. Mary in the hymn had been apart from her family, too. Her baby, Jesus, was born among animals and strangers. Yet the Christmas gospel told of God's sending messengers to celebrate: angels, shepherds, wise men. *God*, I prayed, *please send someone to Auntie tonight to help her not be lonely.*

'Tis Christ our God,
Who far on high,
Had heard your sad
And bitter cry.

Had God heard Auntie's sad cries? Why was she still not well? Before the end of the third verse, the men were already blowing out the dangerously short candles.

After the hymn ended, there was loud knocking on the front door. Mr. Pekkonen let in the visitor and the little girls' eyes saucered. It was Joulupukki! The white-bearded man in a long red coat trimmed with white asked, "*Onko täällä kilttejä lapsia?* Are there any nice children here?"

Mandi scuttled to her mother and cowered behind her skirts. I swept up Sanni and faced Joulupukki, saying, "*Kyllä on!* Yes, indeed!"

Helena grasped Mandi's hand and dragged her over to join us. John and Helena said in unison, "*Kyllä on!*" Joulupukki reached into his sack to pull out candies and oranges. Sanni "gave" me hers.

Mrs. Pekkonen served coffee, *pulla*, and cookies in the

parlour. Unbelievably, my stomach had room again, and I managed to eat one of everything. John wolfed down twice that amount. Helena and I fed the babies their milk and settled them to sleep.

Returning to the parlour, we found the conversation had turned, as usual, to the war overseas. After the adults discussed whether the Germans could be kept from invading England, they moved on to talking about the "old days in Finland." Our parents shared some memories that had us laughing, and others that had the ladies dabbing their shiny eyes with handkerchiefs. A few Finnish boarders joined in to sing songs from the Old Country. John, half asleep and utterly bored, asked, "Aren't there any happy songs in Finland?"

He was ignored and the singing continued. Helena, John, and I studied a jigsaw puzzle partially assembled on a corner table. We couldn't attach any of the loose pieces. John whined, claiming he wanted to play Parcheesi, but gave up ten minutes into the game. Finally my parents were ready to go home.

"*Hauskaa Joulua!*" we called out in farewell. "Merry Christmas!"

Uncle Arvo arrived an hour before New Year's Eve dinner. He pulled up in his sleigh with Copper's bells jangling.

"Hello, Saara," he called as I stepped outside the porch. Together we unharnessed Copper. I brushed her shaggy reddish-brown coat while Uncle spread hay in the manger. His face looked thinner than I remembered.

"How are Ace and the cows?" I asked. Caring for the

cows was women's work, so Auntie had always looked after them.

"Mr. Koski has been keeping Ace fit skidding logs from his woodlot. The cows? Well, the good news is none of them have bovine tuberculosis. The bad news is they won't stop kicking with my clumsy hands milking them." He made a slight choking sound. "We all want Marja back, don't we?"

I nodded. Uncle blew out air like a blacksmith's bellows and we headed indoors. Sanni's smile for her father wasn't because she remembered him—she smiled for any human face these days. But I let him think she recognized him.

Helena and her family joined us for dinner. In his loud, jolly way, Mr. Pekkonen greeted Uncle. "Arvo—it's good to see you." He shook Uncle's hand. "How is your lovely wife keeping?"

Uncle stared at him and swallowed. He managed to croak, "She's slowly improving."

"That's heading in the right direction," said Mr. Pekkonen, slapping him on the back.

Helena squeezed my hand, whispering, "I wish your aunt could be here." I squeezed back. *Me, too.*

Thoughts of Aunt Marja spread like a fog around and through us. It had no effect on John, though. He started grinning, saying, "Does anybody know why gorillas have such big nostrils?"

"To locate their food by smell?" asked Papa.

"No." John chuckled. "It's because they have such big fingers."

"Jussi, that's crude," admonished Mama, yet she joined in the laughter.

John's humour dispelled the gloomy fog. Uncle lightened up, saying, "Week before last a new immigrant worker showed up late for supper at the cookhouse. The cook told him to serve himself some cold thickened fruit soup. In the dim lantern light, the man found the wrong pot. He filled his bowl and added cream. Each spoonful he ate made his face contort, but he ate it all. Can you guess what it was? Leftover pork and beans!"

I grimaced and laughed. Mr. Pekkonen and Uncle Arvo entertained us with stories they'd heard at different lumber camps.

At midnight, Helena's father insisted on telling our fortunes with molten lead. The Finnish custom had held such promise for me last year with the cooling metal forming the shape of a boat: a travelling year. My journey had taken me further than I ever could have imagined. Why not try again for nineteen hundred and fifteen? As I was about to step forward, Uncle beat me to it.

"I've been looking forward to this night, hoping for a promising sign," he said.

Mr. Pekkonen melted a piece of lead and plunged it in cold water. *Sizzle. Sputter. Clunk.* Fishing out the lump with tongs, he hemmed and hawed, turning the metal over several times. "This one has me stumped, Arvo. My best guess is it's a house or a shed, but I have no clue what it could mean."

"Perhaps it symbolizes the farmhouse and a return to normal life," said Helena's mother. "We're praying for that. Others would have given in to despair by now, Arvo, and be full of either resentment or liquor. But you keep on hoping. You're a good man."

Uncle said nothing, his lips set in a straight line.

Mr. Pekkonen patted Uncle's shoulder, then returned to the stove. "Who's next? Saara?"

"Yes, please." *Be a crown fit for a princess*, I pleaded. Then I'd know I'd get the part of Aedgiva.

Hiss. Plunk. The lead sank to the bottom of the pail.

"No doubt about this one, miss." He held out the lead with the tongs. The shape wasn't a crown. It wasn't a boat.

"Now we know where you belong," teased John.

I was tempted to kick him in the shin. The lead wasn't anything but a common kitchen bench. What a stupid custom. I thought my life had been spared for a grand purpose. I was wrong. I'd be stuck with dreaded kitchen chores *forever*.

12

From the moment Miss Rodgers handed out the parts of the play on the first day of school after Christmas, I spent my free time practising Aedgiva's monologue for the audition. Only a letter from Auntie could interrupt my preparation for the play. On the twelfth of January I received two. The Christmas mail must have been plugging the postal system.

December 26, 1914

Dearest Saara,

    I can't believe my little Sanni is sitting on her own already and has such big hands. Thank you for the handprints and the lock of her soft gingery hair. What a thoughtful girl you are. The prints are pinned to the wall near my bed. I also appreciate the treats (especially the cardamom cookies) and the thick woollen socks your mother made. Right away I slipped them over top of the two pairs I had on. We must spend part of every day bundled in blankets lying on reclined chairs outdoors taking the "fresh air cure." We had our first snowfall. There are open fires in fireplaces throughout the building, but I'm perpetually chilled since the windows are never closed.

The Blackwells visited me again last Sunday. They are wonderful people, but I can't help thinking about how they lost their daughter. My own Sanni is lost to me, but at least I know she's alive and healthy. I feel such peace when Mr. Blackwell prays for me. There are many dedicated volunteers at the sanatorium, but the Salvation Army folks have a special warmth. They brighten my days and give me hope.

Was that true? I wished I could stop doubting Auntie.

Did you notice the Christmas seal on the envelope? We were given a few each. They're sold to raise funds for sanatoriums.

In my haste to read her letter, I hadn't noticed the seal. I retrieved the envelope for a close look. The seal bore the symbol of the tuberculosis association—a red double-barred cross—and a wreath of holly with the words "Christmas Greetings and Good Health." I wished the message were true for Auntie.

The staff and volunteers spared no effort to make our Christmas festive. A group of church women sewed flannelette nightgowns for the female patients. There were gifts of mittens and sweaters, too. Yesterday we were served Christmas dinner, complete with turkey and cranberry sauce, and the strangest sweets I've ever tasted ~ plum pudding and mince pie. It didn't matter what there was to eat. All I really wanted was to be with my family. Neither the soldiers nor I made it home for Christmas. Which of us will get home first? Forgive my selfishness, but I beg God that it will be me.

Give my baby lots of cuddles and kisses from me.
Love,
Aunt Marja

January 1, 1915

Dearest Saara,

What a lot has changed in one year since our happy New Year's Eve celebration at the homestead. If I could be home, I'd never again complain about the frigid morning trip to milk the cows or the monotony of eating preserved meat. I ache for my little girl, my dear husband, and the routines of the farm. Of course, I long to see you and your family, as well.

My roommates enjoyed a taste of the precious cardamom cookies, but the nurses refused my offer. It was difficult for me to share, and their rudeness hurt. At first I thought it was because I'm an immigrant. Or they thought I might poison them. Bless dear Josephine for persisting in explaining to me the rules the nurses must abide by. They are forbidden to accept any food or candy from any patient.

Speaking of food, we're getting used to the changes because of wartime shortages. The cooks use more whole wheat flour. There's no more white sugar, so I put brown sugar in my coffee (it improves the taste). Thank heavens we have the piggery and hennery to keep us supplied with meat and eggs.

Do you remember our dear nurse Miss Hardy? She wrote from France, where she's one of the "Bluebirds" nursing in a hotel-turned-hospital. During one night the number of patients sent to them filled half the wards. I won't bore you with her details of their wounds, but she said trench foot (from standing in mud) caused the most grievous suffering. Miss Hardy met a nurse who was born in Port Arthur and asked if I knew her. It made me laugh. She must think Port Arthur is a mere village. It was sweet of her to take the time to write to us and to "wish that we would be heaps better."

May your audition be a success and your dream come true.

Love,
Aunt Marja

I hoped in my next letter to Auntie I could tell her I'd had a successful audition. I smiled, thinking how that news would lift her spirits.

The big day finally arrived. Senja, Doris, and I were auditioning for the lead female role. My confidence soared. Surely Miss Rodgers would choose me to be Aedgiva. That morning she'd selected Richard to play Aedgiva's brother Rupert. Having to work closely with Richard wasn't as unappealing as it used to be. Lately his teasing was less cruel and more witty. He'd also started paying attention to the school nurse's hygiene lesson.

I should have eaten lunch, but I was full of jitters. It was my turn, and my stomach rumbled and growled. Stepping to the front of the classroom, I closed my eyes briefly. I focused on the monologue, slowing my breathing.

"Your Majesty, Father," I began, adding a curtsy and a nervous giggle as the script instructed, "and noble gentlemen of the court, I beseech you to hear my request. My fair brother Rupert ..." A giggle rose inside me at calling Richard my fair brother, but I smothered it in time. "... is in grave danger and we must proceed with clever haste to thwart our enemy's intentions."

I clasped my hands, stretched to my full height, and continued. "This very night Rupert will be hung from the gallows if we fail to secure his escape. How do I know of this evil plan? Prepare yourselves for a shocking statement. I, Princess Aedgiva, disguised myself as a peasant lad and infiltrated the enemy camp ..." I waited two beats to allow for their reaction. "... where I positioned myself to hear the pronouncement of Rupert's fate. I entreat you to move swiftly to free my dear brother and heir to the throne." Swooning, I collapsed (safely, as practised) onto the floor in a feigned state of unconsciousness. Of all the actions directed for Aedgiva, that was the one I wanted to change. It was an anticlimax to her heroic escapade and bold plea before the court. It proved effective, however, as my class applauded with gusto.

Senja was called next. She scowled at me on her way past. While her performance matched mine for intensity, she had a shrill edge to her speech. Also, it was odd to hear Aedgiva say "a socking statement" and "heir to te trone." Senja had worked hard to eliminate her Finnish accent since immigrating the year before, but there were certain sounds in English that eluded her. Our classmates had to be given credit for not laughing. Miss Rodgers smiled as she clapped.

Lastly, Doris stood before us, her legs quaking enough to make her skirt ripple. That had happened to me the first few times I gave recitations. She filled her voice with expression and projected it to the back of the room. Partway through, I wondered if Miss Rodgers had noticed the way Doris mixed up the order of some words. In the final line she stumbled on the word "entreat" but ended strongly. She misjudged her faint and grimaced when her head hit the floor. As we applauded for Doris, I was relieved to see her jump up grinning, unhurt.

Miss Rodgers took forever reviewing her notes before telling us her decision. "Thank you, ladies, for your outstanding auditions. I am most impressed by the dramatic talent displayed today. The understudy for the role of Aedgiva is Senja, and in the lead female role is Saara. Rehearsals begin on Tuesday."

I'd done it! I leaped from my desk and hugged Helena. I couldn't wait to tell Papa and write to Auntie.

Richard reached out his hand to shake mine. "Congratulations, Saara. I figured you'd win the part."

"Thank you. And it's no surprise to me that you're Rupert, my 'fair brother.'"

"Why is that?"

"Your audition was the best by far," I replied, blushing. My, I was feeling generous with praise.

"You really think so?"

What have I done? Is he getting the wrong impression? Just in case, I snatched a scribbler off my desk and whacked him on the arm.

After saying goodbye to Helena at her gate, I spied a black-capped chickadee in an old birch. Before the bird could sing its song, I called, "I dee-dee-dee-dee-did it" and chuckled to myself the rest of the way home.

"Awa!" called Sanni when she saw me. I was trying to teach her to say my name. "Awa" was how she said "Saara." I laughed, picked her up, and spun around. She shrieked with glee.

I decided to wait until Papa arrived to share my news. Fidgeting with the dusting rag in the parlour, I kept slipping into the kitchen to peek out the window. What was taking him so long?

Later, by the way he stomped into the porch and let the outside door bang, I knew to wait awhile.

"Emilia, I need coffee." He collapsed onto his chair at the table. "My head is throbbing."

Mama grabbed the stove lifter to remove the circular lid. She poked the fire and added a stick of wood. Replacing the lid, she slid the coffee pot forward to reheat the contents. "What happened, Tauno?"

"Not once, but *twice* today I was next in line for work when the jobs ran out." He slammed his fist on the table. "I came so close." Papa slumped forward on his elbows, his head in his hands. Mama rubbed his back, saying nothing.

Should I tell him my news? Perhaps it would cheer him. In a sunny voice I said, "Papa, I auditioned for our class play and won the lead role." All he did was make a low, throaty sound. His lack of work was nothing new, so why couldn't he rejoice with me? There was no time to dwell on the question. Sipu was hissing. I ran to free her tail from Sanni's clutches.

13

The last week of January threatened to transform us into ice sculptures. To prevent children from getting frost-bitten, school was closed. My one disappointment was having the play rehearsal cancelled. By Thursday, the temperature dipped to forty below. Wind whistled through the tall spruce trees. Our windows sprouted treelike designs in their thick coating of frost.

That morning Mama asked, "Saara, can you mind Sanni for me again?"

"Yes, of course," I answered, and Mama retreated to her sewing machine upstairs. John bounced through the house like an India-rubber ball. Sanni grumped, cutting her third tooth and suffering yet another cold (I prayed with all my heart it wasn't tuberculosis). Now that Her Fussiness could pull herself across the linoleum on her tummy, I built a cozy pillow and blanket nest away from the wood stove.

"There you go, little chick," I said, sitting her in the nest. Sanni gnawed her rattle. As I scrubbed porridge bowls, Sipu meowed from the doorway. My cat skirted crabby Sanni, keeping her tail beyond reach, and curled herself around my legs. I dried my hands and stroked Sipu's silky fur.

John galloped past Sanni, then returned. When he somersaulted around the kitchen table, she stopped mewling to squeal and wave her wiggling fingers at him. John crawled over to her and let her grab his ears. By tickling her under her arms he got her to let go. Judging by the redness of his ears when he ran off, she must have hurt him, but he didn't complain.

"Yes, he'll entertain you, Sanni. But he'll never feed you or change your diaper." It was the most he'd done to help look after her. I loved hearing Sanni chuckle, so I took a break from chores to play. Kneeling in front of her, I hid my face with the tea towel. I whipped it away, saying, "Peekaboo!" She let out a happy squawk. Sanni never tired of the game.

The weather forecast predicted milder temperatures over the weekend: twenty-five below. But Friday was still frigid. Out of sheer boredom from being stuck indoors, I focused on learning from Mama how to bake edible bread. That would at least stop John's teasing about my loaves of bread making better brick walls than sandwiches. I also took time to write an extra-long letter to Auntie. Why hadn't we heard from her in two weeks?

As we walked to church the first Sunday in February, I silently rehearsed Aedgiva's lines to herself on the eve of her perilous journey. *Courage, Daughter of the King. Your heart is true, thus you will prevail in your quest. If but—*

"Hello, Miss Saara."

It was Elias, crossing to my side of Wilson Street. I hadn't seen him since Chief's close call. "Hello, Elias! How's Chief?"

"He's cryin' over me leavin'," he said.

"Are you going to work for another livery?"

"No. The armoury got an urgent call for automobile drivers. I'm off to the front to drive an ambulance car."

Another person I knew was enlisted in the war. Would Helena's father be next? "That's an important job."

"You're right. Too bad the Allies' artillery destroyed only one German ammunition depot last week—if they could get them all, the war'd be over."

I thought to wish him courage for his perilous journey, as Aedgiva would say, but changed my mind. "Well, good luck, Elias. Drive safely."

"Ain't no need to worry about me. It's the horses sent to England I fret over. Dozens of them are dyin' before they even see France—all from standin' too long in mud and water. They'd better not take Chief." He scowled, choking on his words. "Be sure you check on him to see he's well looked after."

"I'll do that, Elias. Goodbye." I hadn't visited Chief in a long time. Had it really been since before Christmas? I carried on to church, catching up to my family. During the hymns and sermon all I could think about was the added terror for wounded soldiers being driven to a hospital by Elias.

As usual, the service ended with announcements. The

pastor gave dates and times for meetings. In a solemn voice he said, "We are saddened to hear of the passing of Mr. Kainulainen due to tuberculosis. The funeral ..."

He kept speaking, but his words didn't register with me. The next day I would see a large black wreath on the Kainulainens' front door when I walked to school. Another Finlander beaten by the White Plague. Mr. Kainulainen had refused to go to a sanatorium, and I was doubly grateful that Aunt Marja was being cared for in one of the best sanatoriums in the world. I focused on that thought, hoping to avoid another nightmare. I had been free of bad dreams for more than a month.

Over a week passed and I still hadn't done what Elias had asked. While I walked to the Star Livery, my thoughts turned to Auntie. Why hadn't she written? I'd expected her to congratulate me on getting the part of Aedgiva. Was the war overseas affecting even mail delivery in Canada?

The latest news predicted Germany's collapse in May, with reports of fierce fighting on east and west fronts. Canadians battled alongside the British in France. Young soldiers like Gordon. It was so hard to imagine. Casualty lists issued by the Militia Department appeared too often for my liking in the *Port Arthur Daily News*. They contained names of the dead and wounded. When would the killing end?

At the livery, I headed toward Chief's stall. Why wasn't he nickering? A stocky buckskin stood inside Chief's stall, looking as though he owned the place. Where was

Chief? I scanned the stable, but there was no sign of him anywhere.

A groom stepped out of an enormous Percheron's stall.

"Excuse me, where have you moved Chief?"

"That snorting black bundle of muscle? Oh, we didn't move him, the government Remount Purchaser did. Chief's been bought and shipped to France to be a war-horse."

Dumbstruck, I reached behind me for the bale of hay so I could sit down. Chief was in the war? Would he be a casualty at the front, too? It began to feel like a nightmare. *Stop*, I ordered myself. Why waste time picturing Chief under attack? I ought to treasure my happy memories of him. And pray for his safety, as I did each night for Gordon and Miss Rodgers's brother and all the local soldiers—and Elias and Josephine's husband and Nurse Hardy … I didn't want my list to get any longer.

Money was getting tight in our household again. The cold snap exhausted our supply of firewood more rapidly than expected. As much as Mama aimed to leave the *Empress* refund untouched, by mid-February she had to use some of it to buy another cord of birch. It was her turn to slump in her chair at the breakfast table.

"I have fewer customers. Most of my jobs are altering suits. People in wartime make do with the clothes they have."

Papa put down his spoon. "In spring there should be more jobs I—"

"But Tauno, we need something *now*."

His eyes blazed. "Don't you think I'm trying?"

"I know you are. The newspaper has several ads for general housework—"

"You earn more as a seamstress—"

"I'm thinking Saara could leave school for a while. She's learned enough housekeeping, I'm sure she could manage."

Leave school? Papa would never agree to that … would he?

"Jussi," snapped Papa, "must you sniffle? Get a handkerchief." John pulled a clean one from the drawer to empty and wipe his nose.

The longer it took Papa to answer Mama, the more concerned I became. I couldn't leave school with the production of *Aedgiva's Quest* underway.

"No, Emilia." He was adamant. "She needs a good education. Over the summer she can work."

"But—"

"You're always telling me not to worry, that God will provide."

"True. It doesn't mean I don't have days when it's hard to have faith."

In the afternoon mail, Mama received a long-awaited letter from Auntie. I studied her face as she read, noting the worried way her eyebrows came together.

Sanni grabbed my chair and pulled herself upright to stand. As soon as she let go of her prop, down she fell, bumping her head and wailing louder than a trumpet.

Mama's eyes never left Auntie's words. I cuddled Sanni and soothed her.

When Mama refolded the letter, I asked, "What did Auntie say?"

She breathed deeply. "Well, she's both sad and happy that Dr. Dobbie allowed Josephine to leave the sanatorium. She watched Josephine reunite with her mother and her infant son ..." Mama's voice croaked. "Marja's healthier in body, but she's more homesick than ever."

CHAPTER

14

I hadn't caught a cold all winter, yet John came down with his second and Sanni her third. Then she developed a fever that turned Mama frantic. Despite the cost, Mama requested a house call from Dr. Koljonen. She was certain Sanni had tuberculosis. He assured us it was a simple cold.

Mama kept John home from school on Monday. When I returned at four o'clock, she thrust a telegram into my hands. "It's about Marja," she said. Her eyes were bloodshot from crying. "Jussi read it and said that a gun went off! But he couldn't figure out all the words."

The paper shook so much I could hardly focus. I swallowed my panic and read:

```
            Toronto, Ont. Mar 1, 1915
Mrs. Maki, 357b Foley Street, Port Arthur,
Ont.
     With conflicted emotions inform you
Marja discharged self will dispatch by
rail tonight God bless.
               Mr. Blackwell
11.20 A.M.
```

There was no mention of a gun. *Oh!* "Discharged"! I almost laughed with relief. John had understood it to mean a pistol had been fired. *Boys.*

"Mama, this is the news we've been waiting for— Auntie is coming home!" Mama gaped, speechless. "Listen."

As I translated the telegram word for word, Mama's mood flipped to jubilation.

"So Marja will be on the train leaving Toronto tonight?" she asked.

"Yes!" Auntie would beat the soldiers home, after all.

Mama pursed her lips, calculating. "That means she'll arrive in the wee hours of the morning on Wednesday. We've got to send word to Arvo. Surely Papa knows where to find a North Branch farmer if one's in town." She scurried about the kitchen gathering the ingredients to bake cardamom cookies. Instead of humming, she sang a joyful Easter hymn.

"May I come along to meet Auntie at the station?"

"No. You'll need to stay home with Sanni and Jussi. But you may skip school on Wednesday so you can see Marja when she wakes up."

Sanni slept soundly overnight Tuesday, but in the darkness I heard Mama and Papa leave in a rented sleigh. As hard as I fought to stay awake for their return, I fell asleep. I opened my eyes to daylight seeping through my curtains, but the house lay still.

The next time I woke, snatches of conversation drifted up from the kitchen through the heating pipes. I bolted downstairs in my nightgown with my grin stretched from one mussed braid to the other.

As I rounded the corner, the kitchen table came into view. There sat Mama, rocking Sanni. Across from her sat Aunt Marja. My heart sank. She was wearing a stark white cheesecloth mask over her mouth and nose.

"Aren't you better?" My throat constricted. "You look so plump and healthy. Why are you wearing a mask?" My voice squeaked.

"Hello, dear Saara. How I wish I could hug you, but I can't yet. I mustn't touch my baby, either." I dropped onto a kitchen chair, unable to stop staring. Auntie continued, "I *am* feeling better, but I'm not completely well yet—still contagious, I'm afraid."

"Why did the doctor let you leave?"

"I didn't give him a choice," said Auntie with a nervous laugh. "I left with treatment instructions, sputum boxes, and disposable cheesecloth masks and handkerchiefs, but without his permission."

"She's old enough to know the truth, Marja," said Mama, getting up to warm Sanni's milk. "Tell her why you left."

"Christmas was torture for me there, the loneliness so bitter I could taste it. The homesickness became unbearable. The day after Josephine left—" Auntie's voice caught in her throat. Taking a deep breath, she continued. "—I was assigned the most ornery, ungrateful so-and-so of a roommate. Her first words were something like"— here she switched to English—"'I says to the doctor, "I ain't goin' to the sanatorium at Weston 'cause that's where

117

people go to die," but he weren't goin' to take no for an answer.'"

Chuckling inwardly over my aunt's imitation of the woman's speech, I marvelled at how comfortable she'd become speaking English. Then the awful part of what she'd said hit me square in the face: *that's where people go to die.*

"They announced they were building a cottage for infants. Having children with tuberculosis on the property was difficult enough. I couldn't stand to have sick babies there, too." We waited for Auntie's coughing fit to subside. "The breaking point for me was learning that forty-five percent of patients there had died—and it is one of the best sanatoriums! I decided if I'm going to die from tuberculosis anyway, I'd rather die at home." Her agitation made her raspy. She sat back to rest and calm her breathing.

"Marja, don't give up hope," pleaded Mama. "You're young and strong. We'll do everything we can to help you through this."

Auntie nodded and gazed into my eyes. "If not for your precious friends, the Blackwells, I wouldn't have had the courage to leave. When they visited me on Sunday with a Finnish domestic to translate, I poured out my desperate longing for home. On Monday they returned and gave me a train ticket home, this dress, and a ride to Union Station. They were a godsend."

I got up to pour myself a cup of tea. Across the hallway in the parlour, bedding lay strewn on the sofa. Auntie must have slept there. John hacked from his bedroom, calling for Mama. She handed Sanni to me before heading upstairs. I sat my cousin on the floor and grabbed a tea towel to play peekaboo. Whenever Sanni giggled, Aunt Marja laughed with pure joy.

Mama returned to the kitchen. In a serious tone, she said, "Marja, even if Jussi didn't have a cold, I can't let you stay here. He gets sick if someone sneezes a block away. Last week a young boy from Fort William succumbed to tuberculosis."

"Emilia, I have no intention of staying here. When Arvo comes, he's taking me home. I've lived too long away from my baby, so I want Sanni to come, too."

"I don't understand. The doctor told you to have no contact with her, and you're too weak to look after yourself, let alone your husband and child."

"That's why I want you to come and live with us."

"What? Leave Saara in charge here? Give up my income? I can't." She shook her head so forcefully her bun came loose. "Don't ask me to do this. We'll find a boarding house where you can stay."

"You know we can't afford that—"

"I have the *Empress* refund—"

"Emilia, please help me live what's left of my life with my family. Please."

Mama opened her mouth to respond but didn't. Would she really go? The idea of having to run the household without Mama overwhelmed me.

That night, the horrible nightmares returned. It had been ages since I'd dreamed about Mama drowning. I woke in the dark, sweaty and whimpering with terror. I sat up in bed, telling myself that Mama was alive and well. But it was hard to convince my anxious dream-self, who trembled at the thought of coping alone.

Common sense told me that Papa's angry moods were fewer since the tragedy, but I imagined they'd become more frequent again when we no longer had money coming in from Mama's sewing. He still had no steady job. And what if John got worse? What if my brother's life was put in danger because I didn't know what to do to help him?

A tiny voice inside me whispered, *You could go instead of Mama.*

NO! I couldn't leave. *Aedgiva's Quest* was in three weeks. I could run the house and cope with Papa and John *and* act in the play.

Again the tiny voice spoke up. *The homestead is your favourite place to be. It would be easier to care for Sanni and Marja than Papa and John.* You *go.*

"Absolutely not!" I answered aloud. I could not surrender the lead role to Senja.

I wrestled with myself until breakfast, reaching no decision.

Uncle Arvo showed up late afternoon. He ignored doctor's orders and embraced his wife, lifting her clear off her feet. Auntie shed happy tears. Mama insisted I take Sanni for a long walk, pulling her behind me in the old wooden sled. "She needs the fresh air," claimed Mama. I knew the real reason was to have me out of earshot so the adults could talk unguarded. *So much for being old enough to know the truth.*

It wasn't until Sanni and I were back home that I realized I'd made my decision. I found Mama alone in the kitchen.

"Where did Auntie go?"

"She's settling in at the boarding house on Banning Street," said Mama as she pulled pans of bread from the oven. "The owner agreed to take her in, but she'll be quarantined to her room."

"Can I visit her?"

"No, Saara. She's highly contagious. I'll bring her meals."

"Will she be quarantined at the farm?"

"Yes. Arvo will convert one of the farm buildings into a cabin for her. When it's ready he'll come for Marja, Sanni, and me."

Steeling myself, I said, "I have a better idea."

"Oh?"

"I'll go instead of you. I can look after Sanni and Aunt Marja."

15

Mama said nothing in response to my suggestion. She studied me over the weekend, often with a skeptical look. She and Papa discussed the options. Helena doubted they would allow me to go. But I knew my family couldn't afford having Mama quit working as a seamstress. Besides, many girls my age had full-time jobs in factories and laundries, even though it wasn't legal. My parents needed to decide soon, before Uncle returned.

On Tuesday after school I asked Mama, "Could you teach me how to make beef stew as tasty as yours?"

If she hadn't already been sitting, I was certain she'd have collapsed in shock. "I never expected to hear you ask that until you were engaged to be married," she said.

I laughed inwardly at the thought of being engaged. I had trouble imagining myself ever having a beau, let alone a husband. "I want to learn as much as possible before Uncle shows up."

"You're determined to go to the farm, aren't you?"

"I'm sure I can manage."

Her expression held a mixture of pride and worry.

She plucked a fifty-cent piece from her coffee-tin bank and held it out to me. "Run down to the Co-Op and get the most stewing beef you can."

At the Co-Op I found a limited selection of beef. Was it hard for the store to obtain meat, or were customers hoarding because of talk of shortages?

"Good afternoon, miss," said the butcher. "What can I get for you?"

I showed him the coin. "As much stewing beef as this will buy, please."

He wrapped the pieces of meat in butcher paper and tied the small bundle with string. At home Mama had me trim and cube the beef, then rewrap it to store in the icebox. While I cleaned up the kitchen, Mama returned to her sewing. Sanni was occupied with empty wooden thread spools in her nest. Mama and I planned to chop vegetables and start the stew early in the morning, as it needed to simmer all day for the best flavour.

"I'll be right back, Bunny," I said to Sanni as I headed down the basement steps with a woven basket. In the cellar, I wasted no time loading it with potatoes, carrots, a turnip, and a tied bunch of onions.

"Here I am," I said, returning to the nest—but where was Sanni? Frantic, I searched the main floor. She'd disappeared! I was in big trouble. "Sanni? Where are you?"

The wood stove squealed. That is, my cousin *behind* the wood stove squealed and said, "Oo!" To her it was another game of peekaboo.

"You rascal. How did you get back there?" I shifted aside the board-stiff frozen pants (brought in from the clothesline to thaw) and hauled Sanni out. After wiping her sooty face and hands with a rag, I sat Sanni back in the nest. She flipped onto her tummy and wriggle-crawled behind the wood stove. Before she could blacken herself again, I grabbed her. I wanted to disobey Mama and run up to the boarding house to tell Auntie. She would laugh and cheer for her daughter. Instead I flew up the stairs to let Mama know about Sanni's new skill. It was no longer safe to leave her in the nest. I'd need to carry her with me or pen her like a lamb.

"Life will never be the same from this moment on," said Mama. "Jussi was younger than Sanni when he started crawling—don't you remember?"

"No, I was four."

Mama led the way downstairs. "What can we do to make the house safe for Sanni?" she quizzed.

"Barricade the wood stove or make her a pen, move everything harmful out of her reach, and—"

"Especially lye balls," she said, pointing to the box of laundry whitener. "Babies have poisoned themselves. Sanni will soon crawl faster and stand more, and she'll start climbing—"

"I know, Mama. The school nurse taught us the stages babies go through. Don't forget to tell Auntie when you bring her supper."

My hands ached by the time the stew was assembled and bubbling the next morning. Mama announced, "Since Marja approves of your going to the farm, Papa and I have decided you can go—on two conditions. One, you must have no direct contact with Marja. Arvo will handle her contaminated dishes and laundry, not you. And two, Mrs. Koski will oversee your care of Sanni. You must follow her instructions exactly. Understood?"

"Yes, Mama. Understood." As painful as it was for me to give up my role as Aedgiva, twice as strong was my relief at not having to take over Mama's role at home.

Sanni waved goodbye to me when I left for school. Helena waited for me by her gate. "Ew—you stink like onions," she said.

"I do?" My nose smelled nothing. "Mama showed me how to make stew this morning."

"What for? You hate cooking."

"That's true, but now I have to learn. Mama agreed that I could go to the farm instead of her."

"How long will you be gone?"

"I don't know."

"I'm going to miss you, Saara." Helena's eyes widened. "You won't go until after *Aedgiva's Quest*, though, right?"

I shrugged. "My uncle will fetch us as soon as he can …"

"That means—"

"I'm afraid so. Senja will be over the moon."

When Miss Rodgers heard my news, she said the oddest thing. "At times the path of one's life must take a sharp twist to reveal one's purpose." She rested her hand on my shoulder. "I admire your courage and loyalty to your family. God's blessings be upon you."

"Thank you."

"I will give you a supply of homework to take with you."

After her regular announcements to the class, Miss Rodgers said, "Due to pressing family circumstances, Saara is stepping down from the role of Aedgiva. Senja will now take her place."

Senja and Edith exchanged grins. Richard prodded my spine with his ruler. "What's going on?"

I whispered, "I'll tell you at recess." But by recess—with the help of much note passing—word had gotten around the whole class.

Richard rushed out the door after me. "This is crazy, Saara. You love acting! Don't leave just to avoid sharing the stage with me."

"That's not it—I have to go. My aunt needs my help."

It was no surprise to see Senja gloating in the playground. Pointing my way, she said, "Here comes the farm-wife-in-training."

Helena leaped at her, standing chin to chin. "Stop right there! This is noble and selfless of Saara. I won't have you insulting my best friend anymore."

Helena had stood up for me! I straightened. *Noble*, she'd said. *Selfless*. Her belief in me made me more confident in my decision.

By two days later, my confidence had vanished. What had I gotten myself into? How long would I need to stay in North Branch? The more Mama taught me in the kitchen, the greater my doubts were that I could handle the cooking at the farm, plus look after Sanni. But I had no choice. I studied how much allspice Mama added to the stew, cream to the turnip loaf, and flour to the

Finnish pancake batter. Recipes unwritten for centuries I madly scribbled in a notebook. I had never worked as intensely on a subject in class.

On the way home from school with Helena and Richard, he asked us to wait outside his house. He ran in and returned with a postcard. "Look at this Field Service postcard from Gordon." It read:

NOTHING is to be written on this side except the date and signature of the sender. Sentences not required may be erased. If anything else is added the post card will be destroyed.

[Postage must be prepaid on any letter or post card addressed to the sender of this card.]

I am quite well.

~~*I have been admitted into hospital*~~

$\left\{\begin{array}{l}\text{sick}\\\text{wounded}\end{array}\right.$ ~~*and am going on well.*~~ ~~*and hope to be discharged soon.*~~

~~*I am being sent down to the base.*~~

I have received your $\left\{\begin{array}{l}\text{letter dated}\\\text{telegram}\\\text{parcel}\end{array}\right.$ _____ ,, _____ ,, *Jan. 26, -19-15*

Letter follows at first opportunity.

~~*I have received no letter from you*~~

$\left\{\begin{array}{l}\text{lately}\\\text{for a long time.}\end{array}\right.$

Signature only $\left.\right\}$ *Gordon Williams*

Date *Feb. 22, -19-15*

"Knowing Gordon, if he had a choice he'd stick to sending these postcards and forget about writing letters. But then he wouldn't have to worry about getting picked off by a German sniper—my mother would shoot him herself." He laughed.

He *actually* laughed.

"Richard!" I exclaimed. "How can you joke about your brother getting shot?"

"Sometimes a joke is all I can handle."

I shook my head, sending Helena a quizzical look. She shrugged. I couldn't wait to move to the homestead and get away from the incessant reminders of war.

We said goodbye to Richard and kept walking homeward. Helena stopped at the Bay Street corner. She stared up the hill. What was so interesting about an ordinary brown squirrel hopping along an electrical wire? Helena focused on the ground and shyly said, "I ... I thought I should ask if ... if you're still interested in Richard."

"*Still* interested? I've never *been* interested in Richard. Why would I be *interested* in someone who laughs about his brother getting shot? It's creepy ..." Helena looked crestfallen. What was wrong?

"Have you heard about the Kuutamo?" she asked, blushing.

"How could I not?" The advertisement for the March 20 "Moonlight Dance" had been running in the newspaper for a few weeks. *Oh, dear.* She was interested in Richard. She *liked* him.

"Richard asked if I would dance with him there."

A wave of jealousy engulfed me, but not because

I wanted Richard for a beau. Selfishly, I didn't want to share my best friend with anyone else. Helena was waiting for me to speak. I struggled to swallow my bitter feelings, saying, "Have … fun."

After our Sunday lunch, Sanni and I sprawled on the parlour floor. I was stacking empty thread spools until the towers tumbled over, while Sanni jammed one partway into her mouth to test out her new teeth. At the sound of sleigh bells, I jumped up to the window. Uncle Arvo. He waved as he strode to the porch. Inside, Uncle tugged my braids, picked up his daughter, and swung her around as she laughed. "Saara, I'm going to fetch Marja. Get your bag packed, won't you? Once Ace has cooled down, all he'll need is a drink of water and we can be on our way to the homestead."

My legs wobbled when I stood, as if they would collapse. The moment had come to leave and I didn't want to go. I had known Uncle was going to come to take us to the farm as soon as the cabin was ready. But I'd kept hoping it would take him long enough for me to still perform as Aedgiva. The full impact of missing that experience hit me. I wanted to howl at the top of my lungs like Sanni. Instead I swallowed hard. "Be brave like Aedgiva," I whispered.

I packed my satchel in minutes, then decided I needed two more things: Mr. Blackwell's letter and my precious silver sugar spoon. It had once belonged to Auntie, but she'd insisted I keep the spoon after I saved it from going down with the *Empress of Ireland*. I tucked the letter and the splotchy brown leather case holding the spoon in my satchel and ran to Helena's to hug her goodbye.

When I got back, Aunt Marja was standing next to the sleigh. Her eyes sparkled above her mask like the snow crystals shining in the sun. "Incredible—I'm finally going home," she exclaimed. I moved to load her bag into the sleigh, but she said, "No, Saara. Remember, you mustn't touch my things."

Struggling to hold back tears, I hugged Mama and nuzzled Sipu goodbye. Uncle helped Auntie aboard. I climbed into the back seat and answered John's wave from the upstairs window. Mama placed Sanni in my arms. She clung to me, anxious over the strangers—her parents—in the sleigh. Papa patted my head, saying, "Take good care of her … of everyone."

Did I truly want the "adventure"? The responsibility? Bile soured my throat.

No.

Yes.

No. I could change my mind and stay home.

But I'd miss out on living at the farm. And the responsibility at home was greater.

Yes.

Ace tossed his head and pulled the lines taut. The sleigh inched forward. With effort, I smiled at Mama as I clasped Sanni to me. We slid along the lane.

"We'll see you at Easter," called Mama after us.

I took deep breaths. Easter was in three weeks. I could survive that long.

16

Once we reached the open countryside, Uncle stared at his wife, leaving the snow-packed road to Ace's experience. He asked for the tenth time, "How are you feeling?"

Auntie chuckled. "Arvo, please relax. I feel fine."

"Still, be careful. I can't face having you leave us again. Toronto's in the same country—same province, even— but it felt as if you'd been swept away to Tasmania."

Ace's bells jingled as the sleigh's runners swished and rasped through the snow. Sanni fell asleep. I tucked her in a blanket nest by my feet, protecting her face from the cold wind with her quilt. I snugged my hand-knitted hat lower on my forehead. Fourteen miles' worth of frozen hills and trees sped past.

When we arrived, Uncle parked the sleigh between the chicken coop and the tall barn. I revelled in the view of the farm. Across the wide yard stood the two-storey log house. To the left, deep snow partially hid the entrance to the root house built into the hill. My gaze turned to the near side of the farmhouse, past the dip-well's bucket and skyward-pointing levered pole, to the sauna.

I breathed contentment. As I was about to collect my dozing cousin, Uncle stopped me. "Leave Sanni to nap. We'll get Marja settled first."

He steered Auntie by the elbow toward her cabin, the shed next to the sauna that he'd emptied and made habitable.

"Wait, Arvo," said Aunt Marja. "It's been such a long time. Let me spend a few minutes in the house. Don't look so worried. I'll keep my mask on and I won't handle anything."

She dawdled along the path, as if reacquainting herself with each leafless angled tree branch in the birch grove. Uncle opened the door, but Auntie broke her promise, running her hand up the smooth wood of the door frame.

Stepping over the threshold, she exclaimed, "You've kept it so tidy and clean."

Uncle's cheeks flared redder than maple leaves in autumn. "You know I'm not tidy. When the neighbour ladies heard you were coming home, they organized a scrubbing bee. Showed up one morning and set to work. They made sure the house was clean and safe for Sanni. Scoured the cabin, too. And stocked the root house."

"At times I've thought us fools for living here in the bush with no family nearby," said Auntie. "But our friends are becoming our family, aren't they?"

"We are blessed, Marja, dear."

They embraced as if they'd forgotten I was standing there. I slipped away to peek at Sanni. She hadn't moved, so I unhitched Ace from the sleigh. I led the workhorse to the barn. Pungent animal smells and Copper's nickering greeted us. The scent of hay awakened happy memories of the summer month I'd lived at the homestead. The way my heart stirred, it felt more like home than my house in the city. I removed Ace's harness and gave him a sip of water. I stood on a stool to brush his back. Clumps of black winter hair floated to the ground as Uncle entered the barn.

"Well done, Saara. You've had a good teacher," he said, winking. "But from now on leave the barn chores to me so you can look after Sanni and the house."

I wished I could take over his work instead. I vowed to get my duties done in time to still help with the horses.

"Come and see Marja's cabin."

A few scraggly icicles clung to the edge of the "cabin's" steep roof. The moss-chinked log shed had a door and small window at the front. Uncle's tools and grain stores had been replaced by a bed, coal oil lamp, washstand, and rough-hewn table with one chair.

"Mrs. Koski sewed the flour-sack curtains and lent us the furniture ..." Uncle stopped. "I'm sorry, Marja. It's nothing fancy—"

"I'd sleep with pigs simply to be home, Arvo. It will do."

"I rigged up this old stove the Seppäläs gave me," he said, lighting the crumpled newspaper beneath the kindling in the firebox. "I don't want you to be cold at night."

"Cold air is better than warm. I'm supposed to let the fire die out and open the windows wide at night."

"There's a single window ..."

"It's all right, Arvo. Thank you for everything you've done. I'm worn out, so I'll rest now." Auntie unpinned her hair and removed her boots before lying down. She pulled her quilt over her shoulders.

Uncle placed a small log in the stove and we went back outside. Sanni whimpered to be fed. Uncle reached into the sleigh and passed her to me. "I pasteurized milk this morning. I'll fetch it from the root house."

What faced me in my aunt's kitchen pressed on my shoulders like a cape made of lead. Sanni cried when I lowered her into the enclosure Uncle had built. I grabbed a round of *näkkileipä* and snapped off a piece for Sanni to chew. Her crying changed to snuffling as she gnawed the dark rye dried bread. I located the pots, wooden spoons, funnel, and tea towels and tied Auntie's flour-sack apron around my waist. Sanni spied her bottle, dropped the *näkkileipä*, and wailed. I had to stop her crying! *Hurry, Uncle!*

I lit a fire in the wood stove. Sanni would be entirely miserable by the time it grew hot enough to heat her milk. When Uncle appeared with a small milk can, I filled her bottle.

"All right, little chick," I cooed, cuddling Sanni. "It's cold, but it'll fill your belly." She latched on to the rubber nipple and sucked with all her strength. Her eyes bulged and she sputtered, dribbling icy milk from her mouth. But she greedily drained the bottle. "Thank you, Sanni. I promise next time the milk will be warm."

Once I changed her diaper, I stowed our clothes, her clean diapers, and the baked goods Mama had sent along. Finding Auntie's sugar bowl, I replaced her plain teaspoon with my *Empress* sugar spoon. It was a symbol of my family's love for me. I wanted it close by to remind me of them.

At the bottom of my satchel I felt a hard lump. It was wrapped in one of John's handkerchiefs. *Ugh! A dirty one!* Gingerly using my fingertips to untie it, I wondered what sort of prank he'd pulled. Out fell the lead kitchen bench from New Year's Eve and a scrap of paper. Why had he kept it? The brief printed message revealed his reason:

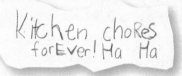

Kitchen choRes forEver! Ha Ha

"Ha, ha, to you, John!" I exclaimed, hurling the items into the flames in the stove.

My stomach growled, ready for supper. *Supper!* I hadn't peeled potatoes yet. Where had the afternoon gone?

I scrambled about the kitchen, grabbing a large pot to fill with water. When the door burst open, I gasped and dropped the pot on my toes. "Ow!"

"Saara, you're here!" called Lila, running to hug me as I hopped on one foot. "Are you all right?"

"I will be, once my toes regain their shape," I said, picking up the pot.

"Didn't Arvo tell you we were bringing supper?" asked Mrs. Koski, carrying two loaves of rye bread.

"No. He—" My tongue froze at the sight of a tall white-blond boy with the clearest blue eyes I'd ever seen.

They were like open windows filling a room with light. He wasn't handsome by Helena's standards, but I liked the way the corners of his mouth crinkled as he grinned. As he walked closer to me, I noticed sawdust and tiny wood shavings clinging to his wool jacket. His arms were overloaded with a wooden box full of blanket-wrapped dishes. Mrs. Koski directed him to where he should set it down.

Lila linked her arm in mine and said, "Saara, this is my cousin Mikko."

He shook my hand and said, "How do you do?" so quickly in English that it sounded like a single word. Finnish alone was spoken among the neighbouring farmers, so why had he greeted me in English?

He gave me an odd look.

I hadn't said anything! "Hello, Mikko," I replied in English. "It's nice to meet you."

The unfamiliar people upset Sanni, so I held her close.

"Isn't Saara pretty, Mikko?" said Lila in Finnish. She spoke under her breath so her mother wouldn't hear.

"Lila," I whispered, blushing. "Don't be silly."

"No silly. Much pretty." Mikko's neck turned red and the flush spread to his cheeks. "I mean, very pretty."

Was he embarrassed at Lila's question or his incorrect English?

Lila jabbed her elbow into my ribs, saying, "I think that was a compliment. Say thank you, silly."

"Thank you, Mikko. How did you learn English?"

"I know little." He switched to Finnish. "We lived in

136

Minnesota for a few months while Father worked in a mine. All the boy next door taught me were bad English words. Father decided farming in fresh air with his brother was a better choice than the mine, so he moved us here where no one speaks English."

"Mikko's sister works as a live-in domestic for a family in Port Arthur," said Lila. Mrs. Koski left for the cabin with a supper tray for Aunt Marja. Lila continued, "As soon as I'm fourteen, I'm moving into town to be a domestic."

In a bitter tone Mikko said, "My sister could learn English from her employer, but she refuses to try."

There was no mention of his mother. I wanted to ask, but what if she'd died? That could be awkward. I'd ask Lila later.

"I smell supper," said Uncle Arvo as he opened the door. "Mikko, Lila, join us."

"Thank you," said Lila, "but my mother said this food is for you. We'll eat at home. See you tomorrow, Saara." Lila hugged me again. "I'm so happy you're here."

"Perhaps you could teach me some *good* English?" asked Mikko, giving me a wink and a wave goodbye.

"I'd be happy to. What about you, Lila?" I asked.

She startled. "Me? Learn English? I can't."

"It would help you get a job as a domestic."

The tug-of-war between fear and desire made her brow furrow. "I suppose so."

Lila sounded uncertain, but Mikko would be an eager student. I smiled at the idea of Miss Mäki, the country schoolteacher.

After changing and feeding Sanni in the morning, I carried her and a basket to the chicken coop. Inside, I collected eggs still warm from the hens.

"OW!" I yelled as the white Leghorn rooster dug his sharp spurs into the back of my leg. I'd forgotten to watch out for him. I slammed the door in his face and wobbling wattle, grateful that Uncle handled feeding the chickens and cleaning their coop.

With our fried-egg breakfast eaten and cleaned up, I dumped laundry soap into the boiler full of heated water. I added white shirts and long underwear and stirred them with Auntie's long stick. Sanni chattered from the nearby pen. *I mustn't forget to wash her diapers, last.*

Standing on a short stool, I repeatedly forced the copper washing plunger to the bottom of the boiler and up again to agitate the clothes and remove the dirt. Although I helped Mama with the chore at home, my muscles felt strained. Unbidden, Aedgiva's lines to the castle laundress spouted from my mouth. "Matilda, is your head a hollow gourd? You have ruined my favourite frock!"

I moaned. My chance for fame was lost. *Aedgiva's Quest* would be performed in a week's time without me.

Sanni's waving arms caught my eye. She pressed her hands together and jerked her arms up and down, babbling as she did so. I laughed. My bright little cousin was imitating me plunging the laundry. Leaving the clothes to boil, I set the big stew pot on the opposite side of the wood stove. Mama's instructions were practically audible as I browned the chunks of beef she'd sent with us.

Later, with the stick, I fished the sopping clothes out of the wash water one at a time. I rested them on the upside-down boiler lid I held in my other hand and let the hot water pour back into the boiler. It took all my concentration not to burn myself. I slid the drained clothes into the metal washtub on the floor, then dumped Uncle's socks and plaid work shirts into the boiler to wash.

Once the washtub was filled, I put on my coat and bundled Sanni against the cold air. I nestled her in her carriage beside the house. A chickadee called from the birch grove. Sanni sang an echo. With uncanny timing, right as I was struggling to get the loaded washtub outside, Lila appeared.

"My mother sent me to help you," she said, grasping one handle of the washtub. Together we hauled the heavy load to the dip-well, where she began to fill the washtub with rinse water.

My curiosity overcame me. "Mikko never mentioned his mother. Where is she?"

"Still in Finland," said Lila, grunting with effort. "The *Titanic* scared her so much that when Mikko, Uncle Harri, and Mikko's sister came to America, his mother and the youngest child stayed behind." We swished the clothes, rinsing them thoroughly. "She was going to come join them eventually, but last year, when your boat went down, she dug in her heels. She would not board a ship to cross the ocean."

To have Lila describe the *Empress of Ireland* as my boat repelled me. Having my arms elbow deep in cold water returned me to the bone-freezing river I'd fought against. Back to the panic and frantic clawing for life. For a moment I couldn't breathe. My shoulders quivered. I stood, shook the water from my arms, then turned the crank while Lila carefully fed the clothes through the wringer.

Lila continued, "Uncle Harri travelled there to bring her and their son to Canada, but she refused to leave. Later he sent them tickets, but they never came. Mikko hounded him to keep trying, but Uncle Harri's given up. He wrote telling her, *I will never come back to Finland*."

"That's a harsh thing to say." I struggled to fathom how he could be separated from his own wife and child. I understood her fear of travelling by ship, but how could she live apart from her husband and two of her children?

My friend squeezed the water out of the last shirt and said, "I can tell Mikko's ashamed of his father's stand. I would be, too. Now there's something peculiar going on. Uncle Harri received a mysterious letter and hid it away. Mikko saw it had a Canadian stamp, but not his sister's handwriting."

We started pegging the laundry to the clothesline.

"Did you get into trouble for leaving school?" Lila asked.

"No. My teacher sent homework along, so I won't get too far behind. The hardest part is missing out on acting in a play." Lila looked interested as I told her about *Aedgiva's Quest*.

"I want to hear more about the play," said Lila, pointing

to the sun high overhead, "but it's time I get back to my chores at home."

"Thank you for your help."

Later, when I brought the frozen clothes inside to thaw and dry, I missed Lila's company.

My simmering stew looked just like Mama's. Wouldn't Auntie and Uncle be impressed. While feeding Sanni mashed stew, she gagged a little. I had her milk heating before she started crying for her bottle. When she began to fuss, I picked her up and pointed to the stove. "Look, Sanni-bunny. Milk is getting warm."

She stared at her bottle in the pot of water and stopped crying. She understood! "What a clever girl."

When Uncle came in to wash up, I told him what Sanni had done. She was guzzling her milk.

"Of course she understood—she's brilliant," he said, winking. "And since she's my daughter, I expect her to be able to ride a horse before she's a year old, as well." I wasn't sure whether that last part was a joke. He loaded the tray for Aunt Marja and left.

While I waited for Uncle to return, I sliced more of Mrs. Koski's rye bread. When he flung open the door, the knife slipped, coming close to stabbing my hand. "You're back soon. Did Auntie finish eating already?"

"She's sleeping, so I decided not to wake her. I'll go back after we've eaten."

I filled two bowls with stew and set them on the table, along with butter, a plate of bread, and a pair of tall glasses brimming with milk.

Uncle sat and bowed his head. "Our Father in Heaven,

we are thankful for your provision. Amen." He loaded his spoon with a cube of meat, chunk of potato, and piece of carrot in broth. "This looks delicious," he said, popping it in his mouth. He tried to hide the wince but I caught it right before he smiled. What was wrong?

With heat creeping up my face, I took a spoonful, chewed, and swallowed, disgusted. It was so salty I coughed. No wonder Sanni had gagged. Uncle gulped his milk. I realized I'd salted the stew twice. I'd also missed another of Mama's important instructions: "Always taste the broth as it cooks." How could I have forgotten something so basic?

I grabbed the kettle to dilute our stew and asked, "Could you please add water to Auntie's stew before she eats?" I didn't want her to cough any more than necessary … or taste my terrible cooking.

CHAPTER

17

After I settled Sanni in her cradle Tuesday evening, there was still enough light to read. I spread out the school work Miss Rodgers had given me. Arithmetic? No, my brain was too tired for numbers. Grammar? Okay. But soon the complicated questions swam in my vision and my head drooped onto my arms.

"Saara," said Uncle Arvo, nudging my shoulder, "your bed is far more comfortable for sleeping."

"Huh?" I sat up straight and rubbed my aching neck. Darkness surrounded the farmhouse. Uncle had lit a lamp. "I must have dozed off. It's too late now to do my homework." I yawned. "Good night."

By Thursday, I was exhausted from housekeeping and minding Sanni. I wanted to stay in bed. We'd had a restless night. As much as I missed working with the animals, I was relieved that Uncle was feeding them and milking the cows and processing the milk in the cream separator. I wondered how I would last another day. Yet we were out of butter.

In a regal stance, I spoke with authority to Sanni. "I, Princess Aedgiva, command the scullery maids to bake bread and prepare fresh butter. Slaughter a calf at once! My brother Rupert is free! A celebratory feast is in order."

Sighing, I stopped acting as Aedgiva and faced my reality. I poured cream into the tall wooden churn. Grasping the handle of the dasher, I pumped it up and down through the cream. Up and down. The monotonous task took an eternity. My hands, reddened and raw from cleaning with strong soap, sprouted blisters.

Eventually the fat started clumping together as butter. My arms and shoulders ached, but I wasn't done. I plunged the dasher into the churn again and again. *Slosh, slosh, slosh.* Sanni grumped, wanting to be cuddled, but I couldn't stop. I sang to her to distract her. The rhythm helped me work. Pull up, push down. Pieces of butter floated to the top. When it was time to drain the buttermilk, my arms felt as if they would separate from their sockets. I washed the butter in a wooden bowl, using a flat paddle to squeeze out the water. Lastly, I worked salt into the butter.

Whew! I collapsed beside Sanni on the floor, letting her yank my braids and gum their tips. How did Mama do all that she did, day after day? There was no time to lounge outdoors tempting the chipmunks to eat bits of stale bread from my hand. No time to groom the horses. I hadn't touched one of the books I'd brought along for pleasure reading.

"Bother," I muttered, remembering I still had to wash the churn.

Before Sanni's fresh-air nap in her carriage that afternoon, I toted her on my hip to the cabin. I peeked through the tiny window and tapped the glass to get Auntie's attention. She waved, got out of bed, and tied a mask over her mouth and nose. After propping the door open, she moved her chair into the doorway so she could watch Sanni. Auntie didn't pin up her hair anymore. Instead she kept it in a single braid down her back. It made her look much older.

"How did you sleep last night?" I asked.

"Quite well. It's marvellous to hear my coughing and no one else's after living in the sanatorium all those months."

I tickled Sanni behind her ears to make her giggle. We played peekaboo with her pink quilt. I spun her around until she squealed with delight. Auntie wiped tears from her eyes and shut the door. I was confused. Didn't she want to see her daughter?

There was no postal delivery to North Branch, so the farmers took turns collecting the settlement's mail in Port Arthur on Fridays. It was Mr. Seppälä's turn today. Lila and Mikko skied to the Seppäläs' farm late in the afternoon to get our mail, stopping by on their way back. There were letters for me and Auntie from Mama. Mine was probably full of instructions and reminders. Aunt Marja also had a letter from Josephine. I was used to mail delivery twice a day in the city; having to wait another whole week felt like waiting a lifetime. When would I hear from

Helena? The Moonlight Dance was the following day. Surely she'd write about that. But then again, did I really want to hear about her evening spent with Richard?

While I made tea, Mikko ripped open the envelope he'd received from his sister. He pulled out a single sheet of stationery. As he unfolded the paper, a small square of newsprint fluttered to the floor. He retrieved it, and his fair eyebrows furrowed as he studied the clipping.

He thrust the tiny paper at Lila. "Look what my father's done now!"

Lila and I bumped heads as we both tried to read the small print. It was from the classified section of the Canadian Finnish newspaper.

```
Farmer seeking strong and busty
old maid (or widow of living or
dead man) to be comrade. Reply
to Harri Koski in care of this
newspaper.
```

Our wide eyes locked. Lila said to Mikko, "I guess your father's hidden letter isn't a mystery anymore." She turned to me and whispered, "What's a widow of a living man?"

I shrugged.

Mikko answered, "A woman who isn't with her husband anymore—either he deserted her, or she left him." He shoved the ad and letter into his pocket and kicked the door frame. "What kind of woman would answer such an ad?" His hands clenched. "How dare he betray my mother?"

Lila and I were speechless. We followed Mikko out.

He jammed his boots into the toe straps of his skis. He speared the snow with his ski poles as he waited for Lila to put her skis on.

"I'm sorry to hear about this, Mikko," I said.

He turned away, his face bright red. "If this is how my father's socialism works, I want nothing to do with it."

As they skied away, I called after them, "Thank you for bringing our mail." Stunned by Mikko's news, I stared at a whisky jack preening its grey feathers in a nearby balsam. Sanni was well bundled and still napping in her carriage, so I delivered Auntie's letters. She asked me to translate Josephine's, standing well away from her, of course.

Toronto
March 8, 1915

Dear Marja,

So, my friend, you've escaped that wretched prison & dashed off home. My last letter to you was returned from Weston with a scrawled message. I've pinned my hopes on my memory of your home address.

My dear husband fights on overseas & I'm crazy with worry over him. Timmy keeps me on my toes as he's become a walking tornado. I fear one day his curiosity will land a vase or platter or bookcase on his darling head before I can prevent the catastrophe. Mother refuses to hide her china, insisting I was never a problem as an infant. But I was a docile lump of pudding compared to my inquisitive go-getter of a wee boy.

I hold great hopes of receiving a letter from you soon.

With affection,
Josephine

How refreshing to hear Aunt Marja chuckle when Josephine called herself a lump of pudding. She asked me to scribe a letter in response. I was more than happy to do something to help.

The following day Auntie wouldn't get out of bed when I brought Sanni by. At first I thought she was asleep and hadn't heard me knocking on the windowpane, so I tapped louder.

She gave a weak wave.

I nudged the cabin door open. She looked haggard. "How are you, Auntie?"

"Not well today."

I closed the door and tucked Sanni in her carriage to nap. Throughout my chores in the farmhouse, I grew more troubled by Auntie's condition. I ran to the barn hoping Uncle was back from cutting trees on his woodlot. Inside, hay dust tickled my nose. I found him brushing Ace in his stall while the massive black horse munched oats from his bucket.

"Come quickly, Uncle," I said. "Auntie refused to get out of bed to see Sanni."

He handed me the brush. "Finish up here. I'll see what's wrong." He hurried out of the barn.

"Hello there, big fella," I said to Ace. "I've missed you." Inhaling his familiar scent, I brushed his hindquarters and legs. His colouring matched Chief's. My thoughts turned to my favourite livery horse. Was Chief already in France—perhaps on the front line? *I miss you, too, Chief. Be safe.*

"Saara," said Uncle, walking toward Ace's stall, "you

have to stop worrying about Marja. All she needs is to rest."

"But she—"

"She'll be fine. How about you help me with the milking?"

He and I each washed up, grabbed a milking stool and pail, and hunkered down beside a cow. Resting my forehead against her warm hide, I began pulling her teats. My fingers were out of practice.

"Don't pull too hard," Uncle cautioned. Even squirts of milk shot into his pail.

I eased off a little and the cow let down her milk, spraying the sides of my pail. I relaxed into a steady rhythm and in no time the pail was filled. After we each milked another cow, Uncle Arvo said, "I'll do the last two. You'd better get supper together."

I wished I could keep working in the barn instead.

On the way back to the farmhouse I couldn't resist peeking into the cabin. Aunt Marja lay on the bed, still in the same position I'd left her in earlier. Why did she have less energy after spending so much time resting?

I dragged myself out of bed Sunday morning in response to Sanni's howl. My eyelids drooped. After she was fed and the porridge was cooking, Uncle returned from the barn. "Good morning, girls," he said.

How could he be so cheerful? I fretted about Aunt Marja. She'd felt so poorly the evening before, she hadn't eaten any supper. "Why isn't Auntie improving now that she's home?"

"The trip from Toronto drained her, and there are no nurses keeping watch, telling her to rest, rest, rest."

"You're so calm. Aren't you concerned about her?"

"Of course I am. The longer Marja stayed in the sanatorium, the more I despaired she'd ever come home." His voice was riddled with anguish. He washed his hands and sank onto a bench. I stood Sanni next to him, and she gripped the edge of the bench and stepped sideways along its length.

Uncle said, "My so-called friends at the lumber camp tried to lure me to town. 'The bootlegger's drink will help you forget your troubles,' they'd say. But the solace whisky gives never lasts. You have to face the raw pain once more, grown larger in the meantime."

I sensed Uncle had more to say, so I sat on the other end of the bench. Sanni shrieked with delight and slapped the top of the bench with an open palm.

"Saara, I've always been healthy and relied on my own strength. But our own power isn't enough when affliction strikes." His eyes glistened. "When I moved back here, I dug out the Bible my mother gave me when I left Finland. There's comfort in its pages, some reminder that God will take care of us. I worry, but I try to pray more."

Uncle bowed his head. After a few silent moments he began preparing Auntie's breakfast tray. "Now to figure out how to get her to eat …"

CHAPTER
18

Auntie became less responsive over the next few days. On Wednesday, I excitedly told her that Sanni had learned to clap. She stared past me, her eyes above the mask expressionless.

"Tell me what's wrong, Auntie."

"Will I ever be a good wife and mother again? My Sanni doesn't know me anymore. Finnish women are supposed to be strong and self-sufficient. What's wrong with me?" Tears welled in her eyes. "When I moved to this farm I was in perfect health. I counted on that never changing, certain that I could survive any hardship ..."

I wasn't sure what to say, but I remembered how Mama had encouraged her. "Give yourself time, Auntie. You will get better."

Was it true? Or had she really come home to die? I shook those bleak thoughts out of my head on my way back to the farmhouse. There had to be some way to cheer her up. Throughout the rest of the day, I puzzled over how to help. Whenever I felt sad, I would write about it in my journal and, like magic, my sadness would be halved. Maybe Auntie could use my journal, since I didn't have time to write in it. But how would that help her feel more a part of Sanni's life? What if Auntie wrote a letter to Sanni? She could tell her the dreams she had for her when she's older. It seemed ridiculous to write a letter to a baby, but it was worth a try.

In the morning I knocked on the cabin door. Auntie lay still on her mattress, staring straight ahead at Sanni's handprints pinned to the wall.

I blurted my idea. She gave me an odd look but didn't say anything. "You're welcome to use my journal to write in …," I said, holding it out.

Aunt Marja accepted my journal, hugging it to her chest. She gave me a weak smile. I felt we'd made a small step forward.

At last I received a letter from Helena—two whole paragraphs. Helena claimed to be "pretty lonesome" without me in Port Arthur, but her letter was full of her activities: the Moonlight Dance, knitting scarves for soldiers, shopping in Fort William with Doris and the other girls, and walking home from school with Richard. Helena wasn't moping around without me. I felt a pang of envy over the fun she was having while I slaved at the farm. When I got home, I'd go on strike against chores for at least a week and do nothing but what I wanted to do.

Helena also wrote, "*I had a grand time skating with Richard. My parents don't allow me to date, so I had to say*

I was going with Doris. Of course Richard 'happened to be there.'" It was impossible to picture them skating as a couple or dancing together. They were too young to be so serious about each other.

The best part of Helena's letter was her writing about how terribly Senja was acting as Aedgiva in rehearsal. The first performance was that night! Would Senja ruin the show? Oh, how I longed to be there in her place.

I woke with a start on Saturday, remembering a searing entry in my journal. I had written it when I was furious with Papa. What if Auntie saw it? I'd die of shame. I had to remove it. But how?

In the late afternoon, Mrs. Koski came by to encourage Marja to go to sauna. She was a firm believer in herbal cures and natural healing, especially through the cleansing sauna steam.

With Auntie out of the way and Sanni asleep, I had my chance. Under the pretense of fetching water, I left Uncle reading and slipped into the cabin. Tying a handkerchief over my mouth and nose like a mask, I tiptoed to the table. The bronze mirror lay on top of my journal. I slid it off, found the offensive journal entry, and carefully tore out the page. Curious to see whether Auntie had written anything yet, I turned to the page where I'd ended off. The rest of the page was blank. Disappointed, I flipped through the remaining pages. Empty—until the last one. Before I could stop myself, my eyes were scanning Auntie's delicate handwriting:

March 26, 1915

Rakas pikku Sanni,

You are nine months old. When you first saw the light of day, I experienced that wonderful joy a mother knows at the birth of her child. But what heartbreak these past months have brought us. A woeful face stares at me in the mirror. It seems the moment we are the happiest, the storms of life destroy it all. Summer's joy dies in the tears of fall.

How your father and I rejoiced when you arrived. We looked forward to a happy life. My fondest dream, to have a daughter, had come true. "Why did the happiness have to end?" I ask God many times. I try to think there is a reason for everything and I will be able to bear the darkest times.

Dear child, you can't imagine how hard it is to lie here in this building separated from you—I can see you but can't touch you. In the mornings I can hear you and it makes my heart ache that someone else is looking after you. You are lacking a mother's love and caring. Was it wrong for me to have a child? No one can look ahead or change what has happened. Sanni dear, you are orphaned now, but you must know you were wanted and are the "fruit of our love."

> *With all my love,*
> *Your mother*

Tears stung my eyes. I set down my journal, replaced the mirror, and fled, stuffing the handkerchief in my pocket. Halfway to the house I remembered to fill the water pails. I carried them into the kitchen. Uncle stoked the fire in the wood stove. The logs crackled and a few sparks leaped out. He stomped on them. I washed my hands thoroughly.

Auntie's words swirled in my head: *lacking a mother's love and caring.* I wasn't Sanni's mother, but wasn't I loving her? And doing my best to care for her? What more could I do? Saddened, I shook my head, trying to make these troublesome questions vanish.

Mrs. Seppälä came to visit Aunt Marja on Sunday afternoon. Out of her basket she withdrew two gleaming loaves of *pulla*. Mrs. Koski had been supplying us with basic bread as I had no time or energy for that task. But to have *pulla*—heaven. I built up the fire and boiled coffee. Mrs. Seppälä carried the loaded tray to the cabin. Uncle placed a bench just inside the open doorway for us.

"Marja, dear," began Mrs. Seppälä, "you're pale. Are you taking any sun?"

"Yes, if I feel up to sitting outdoors. I've spent this week in bed." She nibbled a slice of *pulla* and sipped her coffee.

Mrs. Seppälä pulled a brown glass bottle from her pocket. "I bought this patent medicine for you. The label states it flushes impurities from the body to heal gout, tapeworms, tuberculosis, skin rashes—"

"What quack sold you this?" said Auntie bitterly. "The sanatorium doctor warned us not to be duped by imposters with their vegetable-dye concoctions that do nothing." She coughed into her handkerchief.

Uncle rose and patted his wife's shoulder. "No need to get worked up."

She shook off his hand and snapped, "I'm not worked up!"

Mrs. Seppälä raised her eyebrows and tucked the offending bottle back in her pocket.

Uncle stepped away, saying, "Marja, we all want to help you get well."

"I know," said Auntie between coughs. "Somehow I thought it would be easier to rest here, but it's worse than in the sanatorium. There the long days were broken up by activities, either my own or my roommates'. Here each day is a century."

It was suddenly clear to me: at the sanatorium Auntie couldn't hear or see Sanni. At home she was constantly reminded of what she was missing out on.

Mrs. Seppälä said, "This sickness will pass, dear. Have faith." She stood to leave. "I'll let you rest."

Uncle collected the cups—keeping Auntie's separate—and picked up the tray to take it back to the house. "Come on, Saara. I'll help you wash up."

Several strides away from the cabin, Mrs. Seppälä placed her hand on Uncle's arm and whispered, "Make sure she follows doctor's orders. We don't want another Mrs. Liedgren."

Uncle blanched, looking horrified.

Who was Mrs. Liedgren? And what had happened to her? By the way my uncle had reacted, I didn't want to ask him.

Uncle Arvo kept silent while we washed and dried the dishes.

A knock on the door made me jump. It was Mikko. He looked as though he'd gotten over the worst of his shock from the week before.

"Hello. How are you?" I asked. My fingers wiped the corners of my mouth in case they still held *pulla* crumbs.

"I am ... fine. Ice fissing is good," he said in English. He grinned, holding up a string of perch. "For you." The flavour of the small fish was welcome, despite their many bones. In Mikko's other hand he held a covered dish. He switched to Finnish to say, "My aunt sent this meatloaf along when she heard I was coming over. I can chop firewood, if your uncle needs any help."

"You Koskis are most generous. Thank you." I took the meatloaf and fish and called, "Uncle Arvo?"

He turned from the sink, blinking his dazed look away.

"Could you use a hand chopping wood?"

Uncle nodded and they set off for the woodpile. Mikko worked alongside Uncle for the rest of the afternoon, swinging an axe through the birch logs like a maniac. He also took over half of the barn chores. By the time I had Sanni fed, supper organized, and all but one lamp chimney cleaned, they'd returned to the house, arms burdened with firewood.

"Thank you for the help, Mikko," said Uncle. "We owe you a meal. I'm eating with Marja tonight, but why don't you keep Saara and Sanni company?"

"Is that all right with you, Saara?" asked Mikko, kneeling on the floor beside Sanni.

"Yes." I turned to drain the boiled potatoes. That way I could blame the steam for my rosy cheeks. I dished up two plates of food for Uncle to take to the cabin. He added two glasses of buttermilk to the tray. I held the door for him as he balanced the tray in one hand and a coal oil lamp in the other.

Mikko made loony faces at Sanni, who giggled and snorted. I filled two more plates and glasses and set them on the table. Sanni protested when Mikko stood, but from his chair across from me he continued his facial contortions in her direction.

"I had no idea you were so talented," I said, chuckling.

"You haven't seen anything yet," replied Mikko. "Watch this." He squatted beside his chair and proceeded to stand on his hands. He walked on his hands toward Sanni. She squealed with delight.

His legs wobbled, threatening to crash on top of my cousin. "Careful!" I cried.

Mikko steadied himself straight as a length of Uncle's lumber, then flipped onto his feet, smiling. "I was in complete control. Don't worry."

"I'm impressed. My father would be, too. He's a gymnast. Have you had training?"

"A little in Finland, but I've perfected it on my own." He returned to his chair and loaded his fork with carrots.

I thought about how much I'd perfected Aedgiva's lines and sighed.

"What's wrong?" asked Mikko.

"If I were still in Port Arthur, I would have been on stage at school the last two nights, as Princess Aedgiva." I told him about the play.

"Saara, I must learn English." When Mikko became serious, his voice deepened. "Can you spare some time to teach me?"

"You sound desperate. Why would you need English living here in North Branch?"

"To study horse training and breeding."

"I enjoy working with horses."

He apparently hadn't heard me, as he kept speaking. "More and more people are leaving the city to farm, but as it is, there aren't enough horses in the area to work the land." He laid his fork on his plate and his face became animated. "That's not quite true. There are lots of draft horses, but there's a horse much better suited for the north—"

"The Canadian horse, right?"

"Yes—how did you hear of it?" He sounded surprised.

"Uncle Arvo told me. He called it an 'iron horse' and an 'easy keeper.' He said that it needs less feed and can stay outdoors during the winter."

"You know a lot. The breed came close to extinction, but I've heard it's making a comeback."

"Is it true a Canadian horse can pull a sleigh a hundred miles and be as fresh as before starting out?"

"So they claim. Our Clydesdale mare will foal in a month. After the foal's weaned I'll sell it and buy a Canadian."

"I'd like to see your foal as soon as it's born."

He gave me a puzzled look. "I've never met a girl who's interested in horses. Caring for them is a man's work."

My pulse quickened and I retorted, "Why can't a girl care for horses? I always help with Ace and Copper. Uncle taught me to drive the team, for goodness' sake."

"I meant no offence. I'm saying it's odd, that's all."

"Now you're calling me odd?" *How infuriating.* Did

he think the only useful farm work I could do was in the kitchen?

"No, I … I didn't mean you," said Mikko, his face flushed. "Since you're interested, would you like to watch the birthing?"

"I'd love to—as long as you don't mind my little bunny tagging along." I pointed to Sanni. She picked up the corner of her pink quilt, hid her eyes, and laughed, calling out, "Oo!" and clapping her chubby hands.

Mikko grinned at her antics. "How much longer will you be looking after her?"

"It depends on when my aunt gets better. Some days I wonder if she ever will …"

"Is she doing worse?"

"Each day's different, but most of the time she's got no energy. It's so discouraging."

"Don't misunderstand me, Saara. I hope your aunt's good health returns. But I also hope you'll still be here in the summer to help me with the foal." His smile lit up his face. It gave me an odd feeling inside—a little sick, yet not a bad feeling. Of course I blushed again. Unlike Mikko with his handstand, I was never in control of the shade of my cheeks.

I changed the topic. "Well, Mikko Koski, prepare to be instructed in the English language. Lila's welcome, too. We can start classes on Wednesday afternoon."

"Yes, ma'am. I mean, yes, Miss Mäki. Anything you say, Miss Mäki." He dipped his head in respect. "You're the teacher."

It was my turn to grin.

19

I carried Sanni to the Koskis' on Wednesday afternoon and settled her for her nap. Lila and Mikko returned to the farmhouse with me so we could study undisturbed. I spoke English at first, but Mikko frowned and it looked as if Lila was about to burst into tears. I remembered that Miss Rodgers had allowed a new immigrant in the class to have a student translator, so I switched to Finnish. Mikko and Lila relaxed at the table.

"When you speak English, it sounds like jabbering and gabbling," Lila moaned. "I'll never learn this strange language."

"It takes a little time. Let's try learning the alphabet," I said, "then the letter sounds, and how to pronounce different letter combinations."

Mikko tipped his chair on its back two legs, saying, "I know this already."

"But Lila doesn't. You did say you wanted to learn proper English, didn't you?"

Begrudgingly he nodded.

Lila had brought along pencils and a sheaf of paper.

I printed each letter and said its name, having Mikko and Lila repeat it after me. Their "b" was closer to a "p," but I praised their effort. They did well until we got to "j," which Lila insisted on calling "yay." It was a tricky pronunciation for a Finlander's tongue. The sound of "q" had Lila in stitches.

With "th" I showed them how I rested my tongue against my top front teeth and blew out. Lila tried it and sounded as if she were coughing up a hairball. So far the most difficult part about teaching English was keeping from giggling. Mikko made a noise somewhere between "t" and "th." He drank in my lesson like Ace at the water trough after a day of plowing in the sun.

When Mrs. Koski returned with Sanni, Lila rubbed her forehead and leaped from her chair.

"We're done so soon?" asked Mikko. "Can we continue tomorrow?" I smiled. His eagerness told me I must be doing something right.

"Sanni could nap at our house again," said Lila's mother, "but on Friday I'll need Lila's help to prepare for Easter."

Easter! I clapped my hand over my mouth. How could I have forgotten Easter, with all the special dishes to cook? My family was coming on Saturday and I had to make certain the farmhouse was spotless, too. If I didn't, Mama might make me trade places with her.

"Saara, there's no need to panic," said Mrs. Koski with a laugh. "I'm expecting all of you for Easter dinner on Sunday."

"Thank you!" I said with immense relief.

The next afternoon I took Lila and Mikko through the alphabet once again, naming objects in the kitchen or drawing pictures that started with each letter. For "c" I picked up a cup, then drew Sipu's face and printed C-A-T underneath. Both my students pronounced it perfectly. Beaming, I said in English, "Good job."

"What is 'yob'?" asked Lila.

Mikko shook his head. "Ask in Englis," he hissed. I covered my mouth with my hand to hide the flicker of a smile. He was determined to learn.

Later I walked back to the Koskis' farm with my pupils. I had a knack for teaching. I wondered what Miss Rodgers was teaching the class, now that *Aedgiva's Quest* was over. I missed her spirit of adventure and her challenging me to strive. In preparing and teaching English lessons, I tried to follow her first-rate example.

As we passed their pig pen, Mikko grabbed my arm, pointed at a porker, and confidently stated, "Cat. C-A-T. Cat."

Laughing, I said, "Good joke."

But he stared at me, looking bewildered. "No yoke— it not cat?"

Lila planted her hands on her hips and said in heated Finnish, "Saara, you told us it's called 'cat.'"

"No, I didn't." Where had they gotten that idea from? "It's a pig. P-I-G. Pig."

"Pig," Mikko echoed. In Finnish he said, "Why did you draw a pig and call it 'cat'?"

"Was my cat drawing *that* terrible?"

Lila nodded. I groaned. "No more drawings for me." Maybe I wasn't meant to be a teacher.

"If I did the drawings, maybe that would help me learn," said Lila.

I smiled. "That's a great idea."

We said goodbye and I headed back home with Sanni. As we passed Auntie's cabin, I was surprised to hear Uncle's voice from inside. Farm work usually kept him occupied until suppertime. I paused. What surprised me more was the intensity, the anger, in his speech.

I heard Auntie shout, "You don't care, do you?" followed by sobbing and coughing.

"Marja, you know that's not true," said Uncle.

They continued speaking, but in tones too low for me to discern their words. Aunt Marja's health was worrisome enough. Their quarrel filled me with anxious thoughts.

Before the rooster crowed on Saturday morning, I sprang out of bed—my family was arriving that day. I reviewed my list in my head: shake mats, sweep and scrub the jack pine floors, prepare beds, simmer stew. I wished I could cut a bunch of pussy willows to decorate the house, but spring would be a while coming yet. I hoped that Sanni would not have a cranky day so that I could get the tasks done.

As I worked, my dress kept getting in my way. I dug around in Uncle's room to find a shirt and a pair of his old pants. Far more practical for housework.

On my hands and knees, I scrubbed the pine floor,

thinking of Aedgiva disguised as a peasant lad. "Remember, noble knights, you must protect me," I declared near the wood stove, my trouser-clad backside facing the door. "My true identity must never be revealed."

There was a sharp knock and the door flung open.

"Saara?" exclaimed Mikko. "Is that you?"

Flushed, I turned. Before I could speak, the room filled with a snorting laugh. The sound came from the tall moustached man outside the door. "She's a strange one, pretending to be a boy," he said in a deep voice.

Did Mikko consider me strange, too? Had he heard my lines? The heat of my face notched upward a degree or two.

"I ... I work faster wearing these clothes."

"Father and I are heading to town to pick up supplies," said Mikko, unsuccessful at swallowing his grin. "Do you need anything?"

So the man with Mikko was his father, Harri. I replied with as much dignity as I could muster, "My folks are bringing supplies for us today." Brushing stray hairs away from my eyes, I dripped soapy water on my shirt front. "Thank you, though." As I watched them depart, I vowed to wear a dress from that point on, no matter how much of an impediment it was.

By suppertime I was ready. But where was my family? I was glad I'd made a stew so it would taste fine no matter when we ate. Scooping up Sanni, I headed to the barn to find my uncle.

"Do you think you should go search for them?"

Uncle tousled Sanni's gingery wisps of hair as he

replied, "No. The livery horse could be a slow old plug with the best ones gone to war—"

"But what if their sleigh slid off the road and tipped?"

"Now, Saara. Stop fretting. They'll get here soon."

Sanni reached for her father, and I came close to dropping her. Uncle caught her and swung her up in the air. Joyful baby shrieks filled the stalls and echoed off the high ceiling.

When he handed her back to me, it was obvious her diaper needed changing. My family arrived right when I was in the middle of dealing with a foul mess.

"Saara," called Mama, "we're here."

Sanni squirmed, trying to roll over to see who had spoken. "I'm in the back room, Mama."

"Your stew smells delicious."

"Better stay out there because it smells disgusting in here." I'd gotten used to the chore but still wished I didn't have to do it. After pinning on a fresh diaper, I gathered Sanni and her quilt and opened the window a crack to air out the room. As soon as we entered the kitchen, Mama smothered us both with a hug. Sanni startled and clung to me like a monkey. If she'd had a tail, it would have been wrapped around me, too.

"There, there, little one. Don't you remember your Auntie Emilia?" Mama smiled. "Saara, she is the picture of health." She gestured around the room. "The house is so orderly and clean. I'm astounded."

"I tidied the place for your visit. It's usually in shambles."

"I wasn't certain you could handle the responsibility.

Well done, Daughter," she said, hugging us again.

Mama pointed to a bundle on the table. "There are shoes and two dresses for Sanni that Mandi's outgrown, and a dress I sewed for you."

"Thank you. I won't have to wash clothes for Sanni so often."

"Has Marja eaten supper?"

"No. We were waiting for you." Had Mama come to see me before her sister?

"Show me her dishes. I'll prepare her tray." Mama filled Auntie's bowl with double what she'd eat.

"That's too much stew, Mama."

"Nonsense. Marja needs the nourishment. Let's go."

Once inside the doorway of Aunt Marja's cabin, Mama stifled her gasp. She managed to set the tray on the table without spilling anything. "Marja, dear." She stared at her sister lying on her back in bed.

Mama had always embraced her sister before the White Plague attacked our family. Instead she rested her hand on Auntie's quilt-covered legs. "Are you abiding by the doctor's orders?"

"I have no choice. The fatigue keeps me flat."

"Are you eating enough?" When Auntie glanced at me, Mama asked, "How is Saara's cooking?"

"After the first week, there's been nothing wrong with the food. I have no appetite."

"Try to eat. Your body needs the fuel to battle this disease."

"I'm weary of fighting, Emilia." Auntie's voice wavered as a tear trickled down toward her ear.

"You will triumph if you keep on following the instructions. And you have no need to worry—Saara's a fine housekeeper."

Auntie didn't reply—she was focused on Sanni still clinging to me.

Mama watched the baby as well, saying, "Sanni has certainly bonded to you, hasn't she, Saara?"

I nodded from the entrance. "She tolerates going to Uncle and Mrs. Koski, but she prefers to be with me."

I alone saw Auntie's eyes twinge with a dark emotion. In a strained voice she said, "I couldn't ask for a better substitute."

"Saara!" It was John, calling from the farmyard. I hadn't heard my name pronounced like "Sarah" in ages.

I spun around and answered in English. "Hello, Johnny. What's new?" With a pang, I realized I'd missed my brother.

"I'm a newsboy now and me and Fred sold the most newspapers of all the fellas in Port Arthur."

"Golly, that's impressive." I stepped out into the yard to talk to him.

"*WAR DRAGS ON! STEAMER SUNK BY GERMAN MINE!*" John hollered, sounding just like a newsboy.

"Okay, John. I get it!" I didn't want to hear anything more about the war or sunken ships.

"Did Mama tell you about Papa?"

"No, what happened?" I feared the worst: that he was injured, so he couldn't work, or he'd been arrested for trying to form a union.

"He got a job! It's an every-day, all-day-long job and

it starts on Monday and he found out this afternoon and that's why we're so late." He gulped air.

Papa had found regular work? Picturing him in a full-time job was impossible. "Where will he be working?"

"All over Port Arthur and Fort William. He's working for a contractor."

It was more than a year since my father had lost his job at the mill. The same way I wondered whether Auntie would ever get well, I'd been doubtful that Papa would ever find steady work. It had taken ages, but God had answered my prayers for him. Would He answer my prayers for Auntie?

Papa was in such high spirits he *cheerfully* offered to help Uncle Arvo in the barn. Mama took over in the kitchen, and John chattered non-stop about troop drills and the possibility of German spies in the area. "The Germans might blow up the Nipigon River railway bridge. If they did, telegrams couldn't get through and recruits from the west wouldn't be able to get to Europe."

If Auntie could have joined us in the farmhouse, the day would have been perfect.

At suppertime, Mama went out to keep Auntie company. Papa could see nothing wrong with the world, despite the state of our family and the war. He bantered with my uncle, telling jokes and tall tales, but Uncle wasn't in a humorous mood.

What a relief to have Mama take charge of the kitchen cleanup and Sanni's care. I slouched in a chair by the wood stove, my hands free from mending, letting the comfort of Papa's happiness wash over me.

I drifted off. When my eyes fluttered open, John had been sent to bed and Mama had joined the men.

"*Voi, voi.* My sister looks old before her time. She's far too thin and unwell. Is she overactive?"

"She's staying in the cabin too much. You saw the shelter I built for her so she could take sun. I've seen her out there once."

"She ate so little. Is that common for her?"

"'Fraid so. I can't coax her to take more than a few bites." Uncle threw his hands in the air. "What more can I do?" There was desperation in his voice.

"Saara," said Mama, "go lie down and get some proper sleep."

Curiosity made me dawdle. I lingered inside the bedroom doorway. Straining my ears, I could decipher more of the conversation.

"Marja told me that seeing Sanni and not being allowed to touch her feels like her heart is being ripped out. I wonder if it's better for her to be here rather than in the sanatorium."

"What she needs is rest—I keep hoping she'll sleep more and spend less time lying there worrying."

"It is good to live in hope, Arvo."

"But we're scraping the bottom of the hope barrel." He huffed. "I'm trying to stay strong, but the joy of life has left us. We've quarrelled more in the past three weeks than in our whole time together ..." His words became mumbled. I'd eavesdropped long enough. As I drifted toward sleep, I prayed, *Dear God, please show us how to help Auntie.*

An *Empress of Ireland* dream struck in the night. A girl laughed as water rushed into her cabin. I gasped—it was Lucy-Jane. She said, "Dad, this is a game, right?" Mr. Blackwell shouted, "No, it's real—go!" Lucy-Jane's jolly face warped with fright. Outside the cabin, she lost her father in the chaos of the sinking ship. "You need to find each other!" I cried. But she was gone … drowned. I whimpered and woke up, mourning for my friend. Her father had told me in his letter I was spared for a purpose. If Lucy-Jane had survived, too, it might be easier to believe what he'd written.

20

I slept soundly the rest of the night. If Sanni cried, I didn't hear her. Mama kept her by her bedside and half slept so as to tend to Sanni instantly. Mama was like that—sleeping so lightly she'd hear owls in the dark. What luxury to sleep as long as I needed. And to have no kitchen work waiting for me. And no baby demanding my attention. How did mothers continue non-stop day after day, night after night?

After breakfast I took out paper and pencil to reply to Helena's letter.

North Branch, Ont.
Easter Sunday, 1915

Dear Helena,

I'm sorry I've taken this long to answer your letter. I'm so busy there's no time for homework or reading or writing. Mikko (he's Lila's cousin) ~~begged~~ *asked me to teach him English, so I spend my few spare moments teaching him and Lila. For her, it's painful, and him, well, I've never seen a boy learn so fast.*

Helena, I feel like a grown woman already doing this heavy work. I'm always tired. Some days all I want is to go home and simply be a girl again. With Mama here for Easter, she took over my job. It's a real holiday. I wish she could stay longer.

Baby Sanni loves to crawl around. The other day I turned my back for an instant and she was about to tip the bucket of soaking dirty diapers—vile! I grabbed her and told her, "If you were a filly, I'd hobble you!" I need to figure out some way to keep her safe and let her roam.

I'm dying to know how <u>Aedgiva's Quest</u> turned out. Please write soon and tell me <u>EVERYTHING!</u> I can't wait to go roller skating with you again. I miss you.

Your best friend,
Saara

Papa needed to report to work early Monday morning, so Mrs. Koski arranged our Easter dinner for noon. That way my family could return to Port Arthur before dark. For the special occasion, I wore my new green dress and tied a matching ribbon around the end of each braid. Would Mikko notice?

We set off for Lila's house. Aunt Marja waved to us sadly from her chair in the shelter next to the cabin. The intense warmth of the sun meant the start of the spring thaw. I hoped it would also mean the start of Auntie's full recovery.

We were greeted with a feast of pork roast and gravy, potatoes, carrots, turnip loaf, sweet Easter bread with raisins, and *mämmi*. The malt smell of the *mämmi* made me gag, but Mrs. Koski didn't notice. In fact, she stopped bustling to say, "Saara, you look lovely," as if she were complimenting a lady. I grinned.

Uncle Arvo stepped back outdoors, saying, "I can't leave Marja alone on Easter."

"Wait," said Mrs. Koski, heaping food on two plates to take back with him.

Mama mashed soft vegetables in a bowl and fed Sanni.

"What's keeping Uncle Harri and Mikko?" wondered Lila aloud.

"Perhaps they're finishing that rocking chair they promised to build for us," said Mr. Koski.

"I'll be a *mummu* before I ever rock in that chair, at the rate they've been going," muttered Mrs. Koski. "Well, we can't wait any longer for them. Sit down, everyone, and let's start."

Before taking my place at the table, I sat Sanni on the floor with her favourite toy, which Uncle had made for her. She dumped the wooden blocks out of the small pot and began babbling to each one in turn as she dropped it back inside.

Partway through our meal, the sound of boots outside focused our eyes on the door. A woman's high-pitched voice surprised me. I questioned Lila by arching my eyebrows, but she looked equally mystified. Mikko, Harri, and a blond woman with an ample bosom entered the silent house. Forks lowered, jaws dropped. Sanni tugged on my skirt, anxious to be held. I twisted on the bench in order to slip my arm around her to comfort her.

174

"Hello," said Harri. "Meet my new comrade, Fanni."

"Your wh-what?" stammered Mr. Koski. Hadn't Harri told his own brother his plans?

Harri stroked his dark brown, bushy moustache and said with pride, "She's my comrade, come to live common law."

Dead silence. Mama and Mrs. Koski exchanged looks of disbelief. Mikko stared at his boots.

Fanni gave us a weak smile. "Hello," she said, barely above a whisper. She hurried on to say, "I lost my husband in a mining accident last year. I was preparing to return to Finland when I read Harri's advertisement. I ... I have no family left there and preferred to stay in Canada ..."

Mrs. Koski rose from her stove-side stool and beckoned the newcomer to the table. "Come, Fanni, sit here next to Emilia. This is her husband, Tauno," she said, pointing to Papa, "and their children, Saara and Jussi." She smiled warmly at Fanni as she set a plate and cutlery at her spot.

"*Kiitos paljon*," said Fanni, looking relieved as she took her seat.

How fortunate I was to have family in Canada *and* Finland. Fanni had no one.

After Lila's mother introduced her husband and daughter, she and Lila replenished the serving dishes. The adults began conversing. Sanni felt secure enough to return to her toy.

"Hello, Jussi," said Mikko, nudging my brother over so that he could sit beside me on the bench.

"Call me John."

"Hello, John," said Mikko. His face had been expressionless to that point, but he managed to smile at John, then at me. I willed myself not to blush but, of course, it didn't work. He smelled of fresh pine shavings. Leaning close to my ear, he whispered, "We're late because Fanni refused to come to an *Easter* celebration. Father had to promise she could leave the instant there was anything religious. Turns out she's one of those anti-church socialists!"

I smothered a giggle with my hand, thinking of the "discussion" she and Uncle could have if he were there.

"I'm still steamed at Father," he said, continuing to whisper. "Why did he pretend we were simply going to town for supplies yesterday? He could have warned me *she'd* be there."

I passed him the meat platter. He served himself a generous portion.

"You look pretty," said Mikko in flawless English.

I almost dropped the gravy. "Thank you." I willed my brother to say nothing. He surprised me by keeping his reaction to a grin. When Mikko took the gravy, his fingers grazed mine; the tingling reminded me of the sparks from pulling off a woollen sweater in dry winter air.

After dinner the adults grew sombre debating solutions for the war. There was no end in sight after eight long months of fighting. John and Mikko followed the conversation, but when talk turned to reminiscing about life in Finland, Mikko, Lila, John, and I played card games. Mikko insisted we speak English. Lila rolled her eyes but agreed. I promised myself I wouldn't spoil the fun by correcting Mikko and Lila when they named a card "Yack" or "Qveen" or "tree." We'd work on pronunciation in our next English class.

After the second game of whist, Mikko asked John, "Vat make dis sound?" He snorted and snuffled.

Lila chuckled and said, "Cat." John stared at her as if she were a lunatic. My students forced me to tell him about my poor drawing that had made the lesson go awry. As we laughed, I realized that I'd almost forgotten how to have fun. Life around Uncle and Auntie had become grindingly serious. Thank goodness for Lila and Mikko.

We had to leave before I was ready to go. Mama wanted to spend time with Marja before heading back to Port Arthur. When we arrived at the cabin, Auntie burst into tears. I couldn't bear it and took Sanni to the house. There I felt overcome with guilt for enjoying my friends.

When Mama came to say goodbye, she said, "I'm sorry I can't take over looking after Sanni altogether. I figured that once Papa found a job I could stop sewing and relieve you. But Jussi needs me—"

"That's all right, Mama." Sanni cried in frustration. She was trying to crawl, but the woven rag mat bunched under her tummy. I moved her onto the smooth jack pine floor and straightened the mat.

"Are you sure you can manage?"

"Of course I can."

"Don't you miss going to school," asked Mama, "and spending time with Helena?"

"I've been too busy to think about school. Besides, I'm learning a lot trying to teach English to Mikko and Lila."

She looked skeptical. "I'm fine, Mama. Quite fine," I lied. It was true that I missed school and my friends in Port Arthur more than I'd expected. Mostly, though, I was simply too busy to think much about it. The only reason I'd had time to write to Helena this weekend was because Mama had taken over caring for Sanni.

The following morning, Sanni said "Da-da-da" for the first time. I picked her up and bounded to the cabin.

"Aunt Marja!" I called. Surely Sanni's accomplishment would cheer her. "Listen to her new sound!"

"Da-da-da-da," said Sanni.

Auntie's face paled and she turned her back on us.

I tried not to feel hurt. Why couldn't Auntie find some joy in what Sanni was learning? Didn't she love her own daughter anymore?

At bedtime, I pleaded with Sanni, "You woke me three times last night. Please sleep tonight."

But she was teething *again* and her fussing increased as the night wore on. It took me longer each time to leave my warm bed and rock her back to sleep. When she next awakened, she worked herself into a red-faced rage.

"Stop!" My stern, impatient voice startled Sanni into silence. But in a moment, she was crankier than ever. Nothing I did helped her relax and fall asleep, pushing me to the brink of screaming myself. About to yell, I heard Papa's voice in my mind. He was singing his "Saara song," the one he'd sung to me since I was a tiny baby. Why had I never thought to use it as a lullaby with Sanni? So I sang,

Minä pikku tytölleni
univirren laulan;
Pane pikku simmu kiinni
ja nuku Herran rauhaan.

To my little girl
I will sing a bedtime prayer;
Close your little eyes
and sleep in God's peace.

I repeated it three times before she stopped crying and twice more before her eyes closed. Mine closed seconds later.

I felt utterly drained in the morning. I chided myself, saying, "If women around the world can care for babies, so can you." Pouting, I argued, "But I'm only a girl." I brewed strong tea at breakfast and drank the whole pot.

I decided to ask Mrs. Koski for advice. As we passed the open cabin door, Auntie appeared. "I heard Sanni screaming last night. Why didn't you go to her right away?" She clung to the door frame, her hair dishevelled.

"I'm sorry, Auntie. I'm plumb tired." I shifted my cousin higher over my hip.

"It was a mistake to have you come here! You can't look after my baby like a mother can. I wish you'd leave!" She sobbed and started coughing.

I opened my mouth, thinking I ought to say something, but she slammed the door, leaving me blinking. I was stunned by her tongue-lashing. She didn't trust me? She wanted me to leave? Struggling not to cry, I carried on toward the Koskis' farm.

As I trudged through the sloppy snow, I thought about the summer before last. For the whole month I'd helped out, Auntie and I got along famously. One stifling afternoon we cooked strawberry jam on the outside stove. When the batch was ready for canning, Auntie let me spoon the thick gooey mixture into pint jars. Afterward she looked at my jam-smeared apron and giggled. "Are you certain you weren't butchering chickens?"

I laughed, scraped off a glob, and popped it in my mouth. "Mmm ... delicious chicken innards. Do you want some?"

She pretended to be revolted, but her fake retching switched to hysterical laughter. She felt more like my *sister* than my aunt that day. Our easy companionship made the days fly past.

That had all changed. I dreaded our next encounter.

Lila called from the doorway, looking panic-stricken, "We don't have another lesson, do we?"

"No, not today."

Mrs. Koski joined us, her face rosy and flour streaked. "You look as if you haven't slept in ages. What's wrong, Saara?"

As much as I wanted to blurt the painful reproach by my aunt, I couldn't face their knowing. "That's the problem—I haven't slept much. This little girl is teething and wakes up twice or three times at night." Sanni jabbered, "Da-da-da, schuuu" and drooled down her front. "Do I need to start giving her a bottle of milk at night again?"

Lila's mother picked up Sanni under her arms, testing her weight. Sanni protested, reaching for me. I took her back in my arms.

"What is she now, ten months old? And you're feeding her warm cereal? And mashed food?" I nodded after each question. She inspected Sanni's mouth. "No, she doesn't need night feedings. I'd say her waking is more habit than anything."

"But how do I break her habit?"

"When she cries, you must not pick her up. Sanni needs to learn to settle herself. She's smart. She'll soon figure out it isn't worth her effort. Still, it might take a few nights to get beyond her protests."

"Thank you. I'll try anything."

Lila took hold of her mother's arm. "What if Sanni stays here today and tonight so Saara can get caught up on sleep?"

"Yes, of course. *Voi, voi*. We should have done that sooner. In the Old Country they always say, 'Advice is good; help is better.'"

My wounded heart felt lighter. Auntie wouldn't be able to hear Sanni cry way over at the neighbours' farm. "Thank you both. I couldn't survive without you." The last words came out croaky. I brushed away a tear.

Lila hugged me fiercely while her mother patted my shoulder, saying, "That's what neighbours are for."

I tried to hand Sanni to Mrs. Koski, but she clutched my dress and had to be pried off. Although my cousin's crying intensified, Mrs. Koski assured me Sanni would be all right.

By the time Lila returned Sanni the next morning, I'd boiled coffee, cooked and eaten porridge, and tackled the kitchen messes. For the first time since coming to the farm, I read a few pages in my Junior Fourth reader. I hadn't realized it would be so hard to get to my school work.

I opened the door for Lila. "How was Sanni?" I asked.

"She cried up a storm when my mother refused to pick her up. But eventually she fell asleep. The second time, she gave a yelp in protest and nodded off more quickly."

"That's incredible. We'll see what tonight brings."

"You're to let her chew on a bread crust with supper and feed her extra cereal at bedtime. When she wakes, remember, *do not* pick her up. That's most important. Tonight you can stroke her back and say 'Shhhh,' but tomorrow night, don't touch her. Soothe her only with your voice. The night after that, you aren't to do anything—just let her cry."

The first time Sanni woke in the dark, she bawled. She flapped her arms, begging me to cuddle her. I felt cruel, but I was also desperate for the plan to work. When she stirred the next time, she sounded resigned to her new fate. A half-hearted cry, a doleful moonlit stare, then her eyes closed. It was working. Still, I worried what Auntie would say in the morning.

As I ate breakfast, I relived Auntie's rebuke in anguish. My frustrations and longings worked their way to the surface and festered, like pus in a boil. Auntie must have given up. That's why she wasn't getting better. Didn't she want to be well again? I was sacrificing time at school to help out—couldn't she thank me for once? She never complimented my cooking, yet Uncle said it was tasty. It troubled me that she was so unfeeling toward Sanni. Why should I bother bringing her by for Auntie to see any longer? Why speak to her? Why work so hard trying to please her with my cooking? Anger coursed through my veins—a poison.

I craved a cup of tea. While the kettle rumbled to a boil, I scrubbed the sink with sharp jabs; while the tea steeped, I attacked the few dishes. At the table, I poured steaming tea in a cup and reached for the sugar bowl. The rose on the sugar spoon's handle glinted in a ray of sunlight. It was a reminder of how much my family loved me ... but I wanted Auntie to love me, too.

Dry sobs shook my shoulders. I loathed myself for these hateful thoughts. I had come willingly. I wanted to help. Why was I feeling so resentful, so bitter? I'd gone that route before, choosing to ignore Helena and Papa when they had hurt me. But what purpose had it served? It made life a hundred times worse. *God, I don't know if I can keep going. Please help me do the right thing. Help me to love my aunt, no matter what she says to me or to Sanni.*

My students would arrive any minute. Sanni was napping in her carriage outside. I grabbed Auntie's old mirror with the chipped corner from the drawer and smoothed the hairs that had escaped my braids. Mikko burst in with an English newspaper in hand. "I practise. Listen." He opened it to an article headlined *PM TO ADD MORE TROOPS* and began to read at a halting pace, "Prime Min-is-ter Bor-dem made a state-ment—"

He stopped mid-sentence because I was laughing so hard.

"I'm sorry, Mikko," I said, composing myself. "I've read that our prime minister is a plodding sort of fellow, somewhat boring. Perhaps his name should be 'Boredom,' but it's Borden."

Lila chuckled, but Mikko frowned, failing to appreciate my sense of humour. "May I read, Miss Mäki?"

I straightened my mouth. "By all means, Mr. Koski."

When he finished reading the whole first paragraph, he tossed the newspaper aside.

"Well done, Mikko," I said and began my lesson. He

kept frowning. "Is there a problem with my teaching?" I asked.

Mikko looked at his hands and said, "I'm sorry. Your teaching is fine. I clashed with Father this morning. He ordered me to stop being rude to Fanni. She's pleasant to me, but I don't want her here. I'll never forgive Father for abandoning my mother and brother."

"My parents think he did all he could," said Lila, "that it's her decision to stay in Finland."

Mikko leaped to his feet, knocking his chair over backwards. "Maybe so, but he didn't have to take up with another woman!"

"My parents agree. But they say it's his choice and we should accept Fanni."

"I don't know if I can do that." Mikko forcefully righted his chair. "And just because Father will never go back to see Mother doesn't mean I can't!" he blurted, leaving the house.

Lila's smile baffled me until she asked, "Is class dismissed?"

On Friday it was my turn to receive mail. I ripped open Helena's letter.

Apr. 7

Dear Saara,

At last you wrote to me! John brought me your letter and snickered, saying something about your special new friend with blond hair. That's Mikko, right? Is he handsome? Is he your beau? Oh, Saara, tell me <u>everything</u>!

Yes, as soon as I had time, I would write to Helena and tell her about Mikko. Through a letter she wouldn't be able to see my red cheeks. I could imagine her thinking, *Finally, Saara's growing up.*

It's Easter Break. I missed Composition so much I'm writing a letter (ha, ha). Senja wasn't terrible as Aedgiva,

Drat. I was hoping she would be.

but compared to you she was. You'd have given a stellar performance (as Miss R. would say).

That cheered me. But it couldn't erase my stabbing jealousy. I'd earned the role of Aedgiva. It should have been me on stage, not Senja.

I know you have a far more important "role" there on the homestead.

She was right, yet I didn't want to admit it. Some days the yearning to act in a play instead of performing a grown woman's role was so strong it turned into a soul-deep ache.

You're fortunate living on the farm, away from the war. Here there's never-ending talk of battles and Zeppelin airships bombing England, with newsboys shouting the war headlines.

She thought I was away from war? No. We were in the midst of a war of our own. A war of one. Lila confessed to hearing hushed reports of deaths due to tuberculosis when her father returned from the city. When I played with Sanni outside Auntie's cabin, my goal to bring her joy, it had her crying in the window instead. Sanni didn't know her own mother. No, there were many kinds of war. I did not feel at all fortunate.

Today my father said he was going to enlist. Mama flew into hysterics and dropped a tray of dirty dishes. "Leave the fighting to unmarried men with no children to support," she shouted. "I will not give written consent for you to enlist!" He backed down, for now. Why does war fever have such a strong grip on him?

I'm afraid for Gordon in the trenches. What if he's killed? His sweetheart's eyes are forever red. She told me to make sure Richard doesn't do the same thing to me and sign up (not that I need to worry about that happening soon).

Same thing to her? Did she consider herself Richard's sweetheart? She seemed far more than one year older than I.

Gordon wrote to Richard from "Somewhere in France" (the censors are strict) that he's lost his enthusiasm for the war on account of it dragging on and on. He doesn't regret enlisting, but he's sick of the mud and frozen feet, the rats swarming over him at night, the constant noise of the shelling, the maiming, the corpses—but most of all he's homesick and wants the war to end. It's so horrible and hopeless. There's been one letter from Gordon in the past three months. Miss Rodgers said her brother goes for long stretches with no time to write and no time to sleep.

The one good thing about my letter is its length. I

apologize for such dreary, grey contents. But that's my
life these days. I miss you, Saara. I especially miss your
love of fun and how you can make me laugh. Write back
as soon as you can.

> Your best friend,
> Helena

How strange. Those were the exact things I missed about Helena.

North Branch wasn't large enough to support a school or church. The closest place to hear a sermon was Lappe, two settlements to the west. Our pastor from Port Arthur travelled there a few Sundays a year. We had a service on Sunday that had nothing to do with church or a pastor. Fanni invited the Koskis, Uncle, Sanni, and me for supper.

Before we ate, while everyone else was seated at the table, Harri and Fanni stood before us. Harri cleared his throat. "Like other progressive socialist Finns, Fanni and I are shunning tradition. Today we want to declare our 'free marriage.'" He slipped his arm around her shoulders. "In front of these witnesses, Fanni and I announce our comradeship. Our lives are now joined together, following the laws of nature."

Their "wedding" couldn't have been more different from that of my aunt and uncle. I glanced at Uncle. His arms were crossed, nostrils flared in disapproval. But he kept silent. Mikko's face was stony. He was hurting over Harri's betrayal and my heart went out to him.

After the meal, Harri and Uncle Arvo had a finger-pulling contest. When they linked their index fingers and hauled back, I bet on Harri, the bigger man. To my surprise, Uncle won with ease. Sanni grew more fussy throughout the evening. Unfortunately, we had to leave before Fanni cranked her phonograph and the dancing got underway.

By the end of the week, the muddy roads still weren't passable for wagons, so Mr. Koski rode his bay gelding to collect the mail. He delivered a letter for me from Miss Rodgers. I sat beside Sanni on the floor to read it.

> *South Ward Public School*
> *Cornwall Avenue, Port Arthur*
> *April 14, 1915*

Dear Saara,

You have been on my mind a great deal. I trust that you are well. It is my prayer that you are finding satisfaction and a sense of purpose in caring for your charges. But if that is not the case, if you are discouraged, I want you to consider this question: When you decided to help your relatives there, what did you hope to accomplish by going? Your answer may surprise you. It should help you focus on what is most important.

I miss you in class, Saara. Your eager spirit and curiosity made teaching such a pleasure. Do not worry if you cannot complete the homework. You will have no trouble catching up once you return. The "young men" in Junior Fourth are lessening in maturity as spring

*approaches. Ah, 'tis but another challenge to overcome.
I shall stir up my creativity and find a way to inspire
them to crave learning.*

> *My kindest regards,*
> *Miss Adelina Rodgers*

*P.S. Did you know there is a new War Tax stamp that
must be used starting tomorrow? Stingy me ~ I am
posting a stack of letters today so I can avoid paying an
extra penny each.*

What *had* I hoped to accomplish by coming to the
farm, apart from not having to take on my mother's role at
home? I wanted to care for Sanni so capably that Auntie
could be worry free and focus on regaining her health.
Based on her outburst, I was failing on both counts. I'd
also hoped to become so efficient at the domestic duties
there'd be time left over to help Uncle with barn chores, to
give him more time to log his woodlot. I hadn't met that
goal, either. If Miss Rodgers had intended to encourage
me, it wasn't working. What *had* I accomplished? Grabbing a pencil, I began writing on the back of the letter:

1. I can cook a tasty meal (I'll never double the salt in the stew again).
2. I keep Sanni fed, clean, and safe (astounding).
3. I didn't shrink any clothing while doing laundry.
4. I got Auntie to write letters to Sanni.
5. I'm teaching English to Mikko and Lila.
6. ?

190

22

Uncle Arvo lit the wood stove in the sauna early Saturday afternoon. It was a dismal, grey day. Mrs. Koski arrived later and ushered Auntie into the sauna under protest. She'd already had Auntie in a steam tent many times, to no avail. Breathing vapours from heated tar hadn't made a difference, either. Her last resort was to prick Auntie's back to draw out small amounts of bad blood. The thought of it turned my knees to mush and made my stomach clench. Wouldn't that make Auntie weaker?

I had to find a distraction. Yesterday I'd noticed Auntie busily writing in my journal. It was wrong to snoop, but my curiosity had intensified overnight. Once Sanni was sound asleep in her carriage under the birch trees, I sneaked into the cabin and opened the journal.

April 16, 1915

Rakas pikku Sanni,

My condition is worsening and I may have but a short time to live. I could leave this earth content if it didn't mean leaving you and your father. Sometimes I pray that

*God would take us all three together. But we cannot rule
our own lives or destinies ~ there is a higher power. I
didn't need God in the good times but now when life is the
darkest I know that He is with me. I pray that I can live
long enough so that you, my dear daughter, will have some
memory of your mother. But if that is not to be, I will try
to accept it, no matter how hard it is.*

*I'm thankful that for now you are too young to know
the hardships of life. I pray that your life's journey will be
bright, and if darkness comes, you will have the strength
to bear it. I've had two happy years with Arvo, "eating
soup from the same pot," and my greatest joy was giving
birth to a child.*

*Rakas pikku Sanni, when you read this, your mother
will have been in her grave many years. I hope you are
old enough to appreciate what kind of mother you had
(and that Arvo will tell you more about me). I pray that
you will find some good "parents" ~ your Aunt Emilia
would care for you, and there are many loving relatives in
Finland, too.*

With all my love,
Your mother

I replaced the journal and found refuge in Copper's
stall. Brushing the mare, I considered how Auntie was
feeling. My anger and resentment toward her lessened.
Her morbid thoughts spurred me to pray. *God, don't let
Auntie die yet. Please let this awful procedure help her.* It didn't
matter anymore that she'd lashed out at me. I longed for
her to stay alive. Yes, for my sake, but mainly for Sanni's.

I knew without a doubt my purpose was *not* to be Sanni's mother. That was a role my aunt alone could play.

I waited outside the barn for Mrs. Koski. She said goodbye to Auntie, adding, "May it speed the healing" before heading homeward.

Reminded of what Mrs. Seppälä had said after offering the patent medicine to Auntie, I called, "Mrs. Koski, wait."

She stopped and turned around.

"Who is Mrs. Liedgren?"

She motioned for me to lower my voice. "You mean *was*. Who brought up her name?"

I told her what I knew.

"Have you asked your uncle?"

"No, he paled like he'd seen a ghost when he heard her name."

"You know more than you think. We've agreed to keep this news from Marja." She gazed into the distance, then continued. "The Liedgren homestead is on the eastern edge of North Branch. Mrs. Liedgren died a month ago. Now her husband has abandoned the farm and taken the children back to Finland."

"Oh. I see … ah … what did she die from?"

"What do Finnish farm wives die from most? Tuberculosis." She resumed walking home, then paused. "But don't you worry. Marja's strong. She'll pull through."

I wasn't sure I believed her.

Sanni and I were leaving the chicken coop with a basket of eggs on Monday morning when Copper whinnied after Ace. Sanni jabbered and pointed toward the small fenced area behind the barn where Copper stood under a shelter. Ace was pulling the seeder on his own, as Copper had stepped on a sharp root the day before and needed to rest her injured foot.

"I know, Sanni. You want to see Copper." I set the basket down beside the barn and walked to the shelter. Sanni reached out to pat the horse's neck. My cousin chortled, trying to climb onto Copper's back. I held Sanni high enough to peek over the withers. Perhaps she'd grow to love horses as much as her father and I did.

"Hello," called Mikko. I knew who it was without looking. "Arvo said we could borrow his ladder to fix our roof."

"That's my uncle—always lending his tools, glad to be of help."

Mikko took hold of Copper's halter and stroked the length of her face, laughing. "Looks like Sanni wants to be a jockey. Why don't you let her sit on Copper's back?"

"No, I don't think that's a good idea."

"Oh, come on. It's perfectly safe."

"I don't think so."

"So girls can't be jockeys?"

"That's got nothing to do with this. Of course they can."

Hadn't Uncle once said he expected Sanni to ride a horse before she turned one?

"Oh, okay. Up you go, Bunny," I said, hoisting her tiny body. I gripped her leg with one hand and supported her back with the other. She waved her arms with glee.

Mikko grinned. "Well, I'd better get the ladder and head home," he said, walking toward the tool shed.

"Careful you don't fall off the roof."

He turned around, frowning. "We ought to be working the fields, not patching a small leak. But Fanni insisted so Father agreed." He sighed. "I still don't want her here. Father says she's got a heart as big as a house. But that's what got her in my bad books on Friday."

"What happened?"

"Fanni was milking the cows when I returned to the house with the mail. There was an unexpected package for Father. He said, 'Fanni must've mail-ordered this for me' and unwrapped the box. He should have waited for her to come in from the barn."

"Go on," I prompted.

"Father lifted the lid, and out flew a swarm of honeybees! They attacked him. When he yelled, one stung him on the tongue and he swore a blue streak."

"No! Why didn't she warn him the bees were coming?"

"She wanted to surprise him. Father says she meant well, but I got stung, too."

"That must have been painful."

"My bee stings still hurt and have a wicked itch."

"Did Fanni feel horrible?"

"She did—apologized a hundred times." Mikko paused. "There's one good thing about her living with us—her cooking. No more cans of beans for us." He grimaced, fanning his face, as if clearing stinky air after someone broke wind.

I laughed hard. Sanni joined in with great squeals and arm waving.

Suddenly Copper jumped forward.

I lost my hold on Sanni. She began to slip sideways—away from me!

I leaped to grab her leg but missed. A tiny thud sounded as Sanni's head banged the side of the shelter on her way down onto thick straw.

Mikko hauled Copper away by the halter. I stared at my cousin lying there, a patch of gingery hair bright red with blood. No movement, no sound.

Was she breathing?

Yes! But as I picked her up she flopped like a rag doll. Her face had lost its normal rosy colour. What was wrong with her?

A choking sensation rose up in me, and I froze.

"Saara! Take her to your aunt!" Mikko's shout startled me out of my panic.

"Auntie! HELP!" I yelled as I carried Sanni to the cabin.

Aunt Marja appeared in the doorway, tying on a mask. "What's wrong with Sanni?"

"She hit her head as she fell. She's breathing but not crying."

"Mikko, spread a clean sheet on top of my bed," she said crisply. He did so. Auntie motioned to me. "Lay her down carefully. Support her head."

Without being asked, Mikko said, "I'll go for my aunt and Arvo right away." He ran off.

"Auntie, I'm so sorry. I didn't think there'd be any harm—"

"Stop! Fold that clean mask and press it on her wound."

I did so. The bleeding slowed.

"Where did she fall?"

Auntie's eyes flashed in anger when I explained what had happened.

"I expected her to screech, but she didn't make a sound. I'm sorry. It was a stupid thing—"

"Get clean cloths and warm water."

I was thankful to have something useful to do. My stomach somersaulted with worry for my little cousin. My hands balled into fists. I was furious at Mikko for suggesting I let Sanni sit on Copper. Mad that he'd egged me on when I refused. Angry at myself for putting my cousin in danger.

After collecting the water and cloths, I sped back to the cabin. Auntie had me gently wash the dust and crusty blood off Sanni's head.

Mrs. Koski rushed in and knelt beside the bed. "Has she vomited?"

"No, she hasn't," replied Auntie.

"Convulsed?"

"No."

"Good." The healer's experienced hands felt Sanni's head, neck, limbs, and abdomen.

"SANNI!" she commanded. "WAKE UP, SANNI." My cousin's eyelids fluttered, and her eyes opened partway. "That's enough response for now."

Uncle appeared, sweaty and breathing hard from running from the far field. "Do we take her to Dr. Koljonen?"

"No, Arvo," said Mrs. Koski. "The jostling could worsen the injury. There is nothing broken and the cut on her head isn't worrisome. But she most likely has a concussion. Saara, every few hours—through the night, and all day tomorrow—you must wake her up as I did. Otherwise, let her sleep. Protect her head at all times. Get me right away if she vomits or has a convulsion or cannot be awakened."

That sounded terribly serious to me. I hung my head in shame. "You should never have trusted me to look after Sanni."

"Nonsense, girl," snapped Mrs. Koski on her way out. "We all make mistakes. You've been doing a fine job."

Until the accident. It didn't mean enough coming from Mrs. Koski. I wanted to know what Auntie was thinking. But she kept silent, staring at her daughter.

Uncle sat on the bed next to Auntie. Slipping his arm around her shoulders, he picked up one of Sanni's limp hands and prayed, "Our Father in Heaven, we ask Thee to restore strength to this small, frail body. Please heal her of these maladies …" He continued to hold her hand.

I felt like an intruder, so I stepped outside. Tears blurred my vision. I walked straight into Mikko, who was still panting from fetching Uncle. I pounded his chest hard with both fists. "Why did you tell me to do such a stupid thing?"

He grasped my wrists. "Saara, I—"

Shaking free, I yelled, "You dunderhead! I hate you!"

My hands clenched and stomach knotted. I shouted,

"No more English classes—EVER!" and bolted to the farmhouse.

What had I done? To put Sanni in such danger was unforgivable. I should have listened to my conscience. I burned with shame. It wasn't Mikko's fault—it was all mine. Of course Uncle never meant that Sanni should ride a horse before she turned one. He was teasing me. Just teasing. I was the dunderhead, not Mikko.

Remembering the basket of eggs still sitting by the barn, I fetched it and returned to the kitchen. I wandered aimlessly. I was unable to focus on a task until I thought to make coffee for my aunt and uncle. I set the enamel pot to boil.

Lila flung the door open, saying, "I heard about Sanni." She hugged me and my eyes welled with tears.

"Lila, what if she never moves her arms and legs again? What if her brain is scrambled?" My friend didn't speak. She answered by hugging me more tightly. "I should have stopped at letting her pat Copper." I could have walked away with Sanni still her cheerful, arms-waving, legs-kicking self instead of a pathetic, lifeless-looking bundle. We could have been looking forward to celebrating her first birthday instead of wondering if she'd still be with us then.

The coffee boiled over. Lila and I sprang into action; she whisked the pot off the stove and I grabbed a wet rag to mop the liquid and coffee grounds. She positioned the pot farther back on the stove to finish brewing.

Lila gave me another quick hug. "Sanni's going to be all right."

Oh, how I wanted that to be true. I prepared a tray with two steaming cups of coffee.

When we reached the cabin, Lila waved and kept walking. Nothing had changed inside; nobody had moved. Setting the tray on the table, I served the coffee.

Auntie refused, but Uncle accepted a cup. "Thank you." He blew across the surface, then slurped the hot liquid. "Of all mares I've worked with, Copper's the calmest. She should have been fine having Sanni on her back. Saara, you could never have guessed this would happen. I wouldn't have."

Auntie's red-rimmed eyes met mine.

I waited, but she said nothing. I blinked away tears. "I'm so sorry." I could not forgive myself.

When Uncle finished his coffee, he said, "I'll carry Sanni to the house so you can rest, Marja. Saara and I will take turns watching Sanni through the night."

I roused Sanni after supper. She blinked, stared into my eyes, and mumbled, "Awa." Uncle and I rejoiced over the first sign that she was returning to normal. When we told Auntie, she still shunned me.

Sanni was frighteningly listless over the next three days. She made no effort to move around. I would sit her down to play and she'd collapse. She slept more than usual.

The first time Sanni didn't splay like a newborn foal when I set her down on her hands and knees, I knew she was on the mend. The tension holding my body taut slowly dissolved. Soon she'd be back to crawling everywhere. How could I tether her? What if I made a small harness?

"All right, Bunny. We're off to the barn."

Crows cawed nearby as we picked our way between puddles and mud. Uncle and the team were sowing the oat field. I plunked Sanni down inside Ace's stall lined with fresh straw and bolted the door. Rooting through Uncle's box of old tack, I scrounged for leather straps and buckles. Back in the stall, I crafted a harness that spanned Sanni's middle and fastened securely over her shoulders. She tugged at a buckle. To be certain the harness would remain in place, I decided to leave it on her until nap time. By the time she was ready to sleep, the harness had become as familiar to her as her dress. I wondered how she would react when I first tethered her.

Friday's mail brought an envelope for Aunt Marja. I wrapped Sanni in her quilt and toted her to the cabin.

Rapping on the door, I called, "You have a letter from Josephine."

Auntie sighed and rolled on her side. Her face showed as much excitement as I'd expect from a granite boulder.

I sat in the sunshine on the cabin threshold. Looping one arm around Sanni, I propped her on my lap. She plucked at the yellow fabric flowers in one square of her quilt as if she could pick a bouquet. I shook open the folded paper and began translating aloud:

Toronto
April 12, 1915

Dear Marja,

Thank you for your letter (& thank you to Saara for scribing). Life carries on much the same here. Timmy's growing faster than a willow tree next to a creek & he's getting into mischief at every turn. He tries my patience from dawn 'til bedtime. Yesterday he opened the dresser drawers & climbed them right to the top. I followed the sounds of his squeals & the frightful crashes. He was cavorting on the now-cleared dresser top. Picture frames were on the floor, glass shattered across the linoleum. I must cease procrastinating & tuck away breakable objects.

In my husband's latest letter, he talked about days

of sleet while his battalion was partaking in wretched fighting. He & his best pal—friends since they were toddlers—were caked with mud, sharing a joke, when a shell landed beside them & killed his friend. When the terrible shock wore off he raged. He cursed the enemy, hungry for revenge. I am beside myself with terror that he'll do something rash & I'll lose him. I wish to God this war had never begun. Here I am, blessed with health, having beaten the foe within my body, & my dear husband is consumed by hatred.

I'm crazy with worry, but I must keep going for wee Timmy & do my best by him. Our children need us to be strong, don't they? I read that over & realized my words could make you feel horrid. I didn't mean for them to have that effect, Marja. When your battle with tuberculosis is won, you'll be fit & strong & ready to give dear Sanni what she needs. Please forgive my blunder. You know my heart's desire is for your good health & happiness.

With loads of affection,
Josephine

P.S. I'm sorry for such a dreadful letter—I hope to have better news next time. Keep in mind the lines Miss Hardy loved to quote from Robert Service's poem:

Just draw on your grit; it's so easy to quit:
It's the keeping-your-chin-up that's hard ...
Just have one more try—it's dead easy to die,
It's the keeping-on-living that's hard.

I looked up from the letter, hoping Auntie would be encouraged by these words from her friend. But she had already turned to face the wall—a signal for me to depart. So much for cheering her up.

Sanni gradually regained strength and interest in food. It was a full ten days after her accident that she finally had confidence to stand again. She again reminded me of a newborn foal—which in turn reminded me of Mikko's promise to let me watch his foal being born. It should be happening any time now. Would *he* remember? We hadn't spoken since I'd told him I hated him. Did he hate me for my angry words?

On our way to gather eggs, Sanni yanked my chin in the direction she wanted me to look. She pointed to a red-breasted bird hopping in the grass, hunting for worms. I pushed the cabin door open, saying, "Auntie, we saw the first robin." Would she break her silence and speak to me?

"Mama," said Sanni.

Aunt Marja's face brightened and then fell. Sanni was looking at me as she spoke.

"Auntie, Sanni calls me 'Awa,'" I said. "I'm teaching her to say 'Mama' for you."

Even if she wanted to, Aunt Marja couldn't squeeze a word out. Coughs racked her frail body. Her pillow slip was soaked with sweat. There were dark flecks, too—was it blood?

While Sanni napped, I returned to visit Auntie. She was asleep, her breathing uneven and hoarse. She'd eaten nothing for supper the night before. Was she dying? I could not stop thinking of Mrs. Liedgren. As I padded away, sunlight glinted off an object on the floor. I bent over to inspect it and startled. A shard of glass. Looking farther under the bed, I recognized the bronze mirror, smashed into pieces.

I hurried to the barn to find Uncle and found only livestock. I snatched Sanni from her carriage and walked as fast as possible to see Mrs. Koski. I described Auntie's condition. She grabbed her satchel of cures, saying, "Bring boiling water to the cabin," and raced ahead of me.

After delivering the steaming water, I retreated with Sanni to the farmhouse. It was long after I bathed Sanni and washed her diapers that Mrs. Koski emerged, wiping her brow. I draped the last diaper over the clothesline and strode to face her and my fear. "How is she?"

"The willow-bark tea brought down the fever, so she's resting comfortably. In her delirium she kept saying, 'Not like Frances.'"

"She shared a room with Frances in the sanatorium."

"Yes, she told me so when the fever broke. Marja's convinced she has miliary tuberculosis, like Frances, with the bacteria spreading through her bloodstream. Her fever was stubborn, but it came down. I think I convinced her she's in the clear." She pulled a folded page of my journal from her apron pocket. "Where is Arvo?"

"He's out in the fields."

"Promise me you'll give this to him," she said, handing me the paper. "Marja insisted I take it. But tell Arvo this note won't be needed for a long, long time."

I took the note from her. "Thank you for helping Auntie."

"It's my calling," she replied. "Sanni's looking much better. Another few days, she'll be as good as new."

I felt relieved but had to ask her about another worry. "No matter what Sanni learns to do, Auntie doesn't want to hear about it."

Mrs. Koski frowned. "It's difficult for Marja, but don't stop telling her about Sanni. She must have something to hope for." As she scurried away, she called back, "Don't forget the note."

What was written on the paper? It wasn't in a sealed envelope, and Mrs. Koski hadn't said I was forbidden to read it, so ... of course, I started reading.

"NO!" I yelped, dropping the paper as if it were in flames. It contained instructions for Auntie's funeral and burial near the birch grove.

I gave the note to Uncle at supper. He read it and rushed to the cabin, forgetting the tray of food. I carried it after him, but at the sound of my aunt and uncle raising their voices at each other, I turned back. When Uncle returned to the farmhouse, his face was white.

24

Sanni laughed the next morning—the first time since her accident. She was tethered to the table leg, wearing her harness, and grabbed the bench to pull herself upright. Sanni let go, laughed, and took a step. Her first step! I ran to hug her before she fell.

"Good girl, Sanni!" I exclaimed. I untethered her, then wrapped her quilt around her and flew with her in my arms to tell Auntie about her new skill. We skipped through the open door. Aunt Marja had it ajar for the breeze. But she wasn't inside. She was likely in the outhouse. I waited, certain our exciting news would be a balm for her. If she could see Sanni take a step, perhaps she would forgive me.

Auntie should have returned. No one would stay in the smelly outhouse *that* long. Sure enough, I found the outside latch on the outhouse door secured. Was she sitting in the shelter in the rain? No, it was vacant. The sauna wasn't lit, but I checked there anyway. Not there. She wasn't strong enough to go far. Since we'd come from the house I ruled out that end of the farm.

We headed to the chicken coop. Hens squawked and flapped when I opened the door. She wasn't there. Copper nickered when we entered the barn, but there was no response when I hollered for Auntie.

In case she'd slipped back into the cabin while I was searching, I glanced through the doorway. No Auntie. There was my journal on the table, open to another letter Aunt Marja had written. I shouldn't have looked, but it had become a habit. I picked it up.

April 25, 1915

Rakas pikku Sanni,

The same dark days continue. How different our lives would have been if I were healthy. But I am not and I fear death is near. All I can do is lie here and wait for it. No one can know the heartache except those who have experienced it themselves. I won't live long enough to see you grow up. But, dear Sanni, I am supposed to be writing to you, not complaining about my situation.

You are afraid of me. I want to hold you close to my heart, but I must not. I see how I am a stranger to you. Your father says you are shy of all strangers ~ I hope you will overcome this and become a brave girl, not afraid of life. I try to have faith that God has a purpose for us and our lives are in His hands, but it seems that God is not taking care of me or you.

With all my love,
Your mother

As I placed the journal back on the table, two loose folded pages slipped out. One had "Arvo" written on the outside, the other, "Saara." For once I had permission to read something Auntie had written in the cabin. It said:

Dear Saara,
  I am leaving. Keep on being a good little mother to Sanni.
      Fare thee well,
          Aunt Marja

Keep on being a good little mother? So Auntie thought I was doing a good job, after all? How strange that she'd pretend not to. But why hadn't she said goodbye if she was leaving, and what did she mean by *leaving*? Was Auntie feeling so unwell she was returning to the sanatorium? But how was she getting to Port Arthur? Uncle Arvo was plowing. If he'd known her plans, he would have taken her to the train station.

With a start, it hit me—if Auntie was going to the sanatorium, why had she left her belongings behind? Where was she? A growing uneasiness covered my arms with gooseflesh.

I shifted Sanni higher on my hip and scooted out the door. "Aunt Marja!"

In the farmyard, I spun in circles, praying for a clue.

Where was she? My heart pounded. Should I go—

Crash! The sound came from the barn. Copper snorted.

I beelined into the barn. Sanni jiggled in my arms.

Copper was pacing, stirring up the dust. She snorted again. Her hoof scraped bare dirt where she'd pawed away the straw. Something had spooked her since we'd been in the barn a few minutes ago.

"Auntie, are you in here?" I inspected each stall and the tack room.

My arms burned with the strain of carrying Sanni for so long. I began shaking so hard my teeth chattered.

Copper kept pawing and snorting. Then she moaned.

Hold on. That wasn't a horse sound. It came from behind the stack of hay bales.

I charged around to the other side.

My aunt lay in a heap, unmoving.

25

"AUNTIE!"

I darted forward. She was sprawled on the ground beside an upended wooden barrel and milking stool. And a length of rope.

Was she still alive?

"Auntie, are you all right?"

She moaned again. Her eyes were open and staring at us, but they looked as lifeless as winter ponds frozen over.

I must get Uncle!

But that would take too long. I had to stay with Auntie.

Why was she out in the barn? What was wrong with her?

Auntie curled up, hugging herself. She looked cold.

I tethered Sanni to a post and spread her quilt over Auntie. I knelt beside her and rubbed her painfully thin arm and back through the warm quilt.

I could think of nothing else to do for her except talk. "Sanni is such a smart girl. She took her first step today!"

Although I felt as if I were talking to a statue, my

mouth kept forming words. I retold Aunt Marja every one of Sanni's accomplishments. "You and Uncle must be so proud of your little daughter."

A flicker of recognition.

I had a powerful urge to disobey Mama and hug Auntie. I had to do something to get through to her.

I chose to take the risk. I embraced my aunt for the first time since she'd been diagnosed with tuberculosis.

She stiffened and tried to pull away.

I held her tightly, stroking her hair, saying, "Won't it be grand when you are well again and you can hold your baby, and play with her, and—"

"I have to go," said Aunt Marja in a monotone voice, pushing me away. "I'll never get—"

"Don't go away, Auntie. You can't leave. Please stay. Your husband wants you here. Your baby wants you here. I want you here."

She rose to her feet, unsteady. Sanni's quilt fell to the ground. "I've been a burden for too long."

"Auntie—listen. You're *not* a burden. We love you and want to help you." How could I get her attention? "I'll be thirteen soon, but *I* can never be Sanni's mother—only *you* can do that. Sanni needs her *mother*. She needs *you*."

Something awakened my aunt. The icy glaze blocking her vision thawed as she looked past me. I turned to see Sanni standing by the post.

Auntie reached out to Sanni, who jabbered and raised her arms to be picked up. "My baby! She's well again." She sobbed. "I can't leave my baby."

I couldn't allow them to have contact and break that

promise to Mama. So I untethered Sanni, picked her up, and moved toward the door. "Come back to the cabin, Auntie. You can watch Sanni walk there. And you can lie down. I'll bring you some tea, okay?"

She hesitated, turning back to look at the barrel.

I persisted. "You're tired, aren't you? It will feel so good to lie down in your bed. Think how soothing hot tea will be."

I kept up my patter for several more minutes until I persuaded Auntie to leave the barn. We headed to the cabin.

Once inside, she unlaced her boots, slipped them off, and curled up on the bed. But her eyes remained wide open, glazing over again.

"No," she blurted, sitting bolt upright. "I have to go."

She reached for her boots. I panicked. I had to make her stay. She had to rest or she'd never beat tuberculosis. Unbidden, the Saara song welled up inside me. With a shaky voice I sang:

Minä pikku tytölleni
univirren laulan ...

Auntie stared at me, listening intently. The song made a connection; her shoulders relaxed. She lowered her head onto the pillow. I sang the lullaby over and over until she fell into a deep sleep.

I carried through with my promise of tea after feeding Sanni and tucking her into her carriage to nap right outside the open cabin door. Should I waken Auntie? No, she needed to rest. I set her cup of tea on the washstand.

Did I dare read the note for my uncle? Hadn't I read too many of Auntie's letters for other people already? But perhaps it would explain what she was thinking. Mama had said I was old enough to know the truth. With tremulous fingers I unfolded the note.

Dearest Arvo,

You have strong faith, but not enough for two. God has forsaken me and I will never be well again. I love you with all my heart and that is why I cannot prolong your suffering. I have been a burden for too long. But I won't be a burden any longer ~ I choose this day to die. Goodbye.

With all my love,

Marja

I choose this day to die? Auntie wasn't leaving for the sanatorium—she was planning to leave the earth!

My heart pummelled my rib cage.

That's what that rope in the barn had been for!

What if she hadn't slipped off the barrel? What if I hadn't found her in time?

I was too stunned to cry. My breath came in ragged gasps. I perched there, my insides in more turmoil than cream in a butter churn.

I hadn't felt that scared since losing my brother in the freezing water when the *Empress* sank. In the river it had been obvious what I had to do: keep searching for him. But I didn't know how to deal with the danger my aunt was in. I didn't understand why she'd chosen to take her own life, and I had no idea how to protect her.

God, show me what to do, I begged.

Auntie slept on. Her tea grew lukewarm, then cold.

Sanni stirred. She needed a diaper change. It would have to wait.

Her whimpers intensified, but I couldn't leave. When they turned into hungry bleats, I slipped outside, keeping my eye on Auntie through the window. I rocked Sanni, letting her wrench and gnaw my braids.

It felt like forever before Ace neighed. Uncle was coming back. I longed to run to meet him. *Patience, Saara. He'll be here soon.*

At the first sight of him, I beckoned and called, "Uncle, I'm so scared for Auntie!"

He flew to her side. She was still asleep and deathly pale. Facing me, he whispered, "What happened?"

I told him everything.

When I finished, he had tears in his eyes. "Where's her letter to me?" Reading his wife's pitiful words crumpled his face. "I never guessed it would come to this." He wadded the letter and hurled it against the door.

"Saara, you did the right thing, distracting Marja from her intentions … and reminding her of what is important …" His voice broke. "… that she's important." He wrapped his arm around my shoulders and squeezed. "Pass Sanni here. Run and get Mrs. Koski."

I sprinted to Lila's house. Mikko was chopping firewood. I called out, "Where's your aunt?"

"In the house—what's wrong?"

I banged on the door, yelling, "Mrs. Koski, come quick!"

She and I scurried toward the cabin. On the way I told her what had happened.

After Mrs. Koski saw Auntie for herself, she shook her head. "I should have seen this coming. I've been so busy attending a rash of births ... but that is no excuse. I'm sorry I didn't arrange a watch for Marja, or at least some regular visits from womenfolk. Battling tuberculosis is a mighty lonely business. The body's but one part of a person; the heart needs healing, too."

She scribbled a note to Mama explaining the situation and asked the Seppäläs to deliver it while they were in Port Arthur the next day for the May Day parade. She sent word to farms throughout North Branch, enlisting help. In no time she'd organized an all-day, all-night watch so a neighbour lady could always keep an eye on Auntie. She told them to keep the cabin door and window open and to sit far away from the bed to avoid catching the disease. When Auntie slept, the farm wife could knit or mend socks; when she was awake, they could talk. Fanni took the first shift.

That night, a vivid dream shook me to the core. The *Empress* was sinking. I hurried along the deck, searching for Mama and John. Frantic. The water gushed into the ship. I saw their backs and pursued them. Mama and John spun to face me. I froze. They wore masks—white masks, like Auntie's. In the dark river below us, people clung to floating hospital beds.

Mama arrived at the farm with the Seppäläs the next evening. She found me first and hugged me so tightly I was certain I'd burst.

"Thank you, Daughter."

It was a huge relief to see her. Mama stayed for several days—long enough to see a change in Auntie. The extra visiting with her sister and the neighbours lifted her spirits and helped improve her health.

On the day Mama was to leave, Auntie said, "I often wish I'd never emigrated from Finland, I miss our family there so much. But after seeing how our neighbours rallied around me, my attitude has changed. This land is full of blessings."

A thump followed by a wail had me picking up my cousin from the ground. I soothed her and brushed the dirt off her hands. Auntie chuckled at Sanni's angry little face, saying, "She's not hurt—she's frustrated that she can't do everything she wants."

As if to prove her mother wrong, Sanni stood and took four steps in a row before falling. I helped her stand again before she cried.

"Get used to bruises on her angelic face," advised Mama. "It's part of her growing up."

News of the sinking of the *Lusitania* reached us two weeks later. A German submarine had torpedoed the passenger steamship. As I kept thinking of the massive loss of life (some twelve hundred—two hundred more than had died on the *Empress*), my nightmares became more frequent. So I tried to focus on Auntie. Her cough was disappearing. She was gaining weight. With renewed interest in life, she planned to sew new clothes for Sanni—and a set of matching dresses for them both. Had Auntie turned the corner on tuberculosis? I prayed it was so.

26

On Victoria Day, when Uncle finished sowing barley, he announced it was time for Aunt Marja to revisit Dr. Koljonen. We left early the next morning.

Spring erupted in birdsong and yellow daffodils. Brilliant green leaves sprouted on trees, and white pin cherry blossoms dotted the countryside.

As we drove down the streets of Port Arthur, I wondered at the number of wagon drivers wearing black arm bands. At the next intersection, a newsboy bellowed, "*LOCAL RECRUIT LATEST WAR CASUALTY!*" How could I be so dense? A wave of guilt washed over me at having forgotten the fighting in Europe. Deaths were mounting. I desperately hoped the casualty wasn't Gordon.

We stopped at Dr. Koljonen's office and found him in. He agreed to examine Aunt Marja at once and test her sputum. Uncle waited for Auntie while I strolled along Bay Street carrying Sanni. As we passed a young Indian woman, her papoose on her back, she and I smiled at each other, admiring the babies. The city noises were louder than I remembered, the traffic more congested, the gasoline odours stronger, the residents more anxious.

When we returned to Machar Avenue, my aunt and uncle were already perched on the wagon's seat. Uncle Arvo smiled. "According to what the doctor could hear through his stethoscope, Marja's lungs are much better."

I danced a wild jig of happiness with Sanni. Auntie giggled.

Uncle held Sanni while I climbed aboard. He passed her back to me.

Auntie said over her shoulder, "We'll find out later today if I'm still infectious."

Mama must have been treadling her sewing machine overlooking the lane because she appeared outside as soon as Uncle pulled the reins and called, "Whoa!"

"What a surprise," she exclaimed.

With a lightness in Auntie's voice I hadn't heard in ages, she gushed her news.

"I can't wait to give you a big hug," said Mama, reaching for Sanni.

I climbed down and Sipu purred, rubbing against my legs. I cuddled her, nuzzling her soft furry side.

After lunch, Uncle left to pick up supplies, Sanni napped, and the ladies visited. The hour hand on the clock took forever to reach four. It was time to head to Helena's house. I smoothed my mussed braids and bounded down the steep lane. Mrs. Pekkonen exclaimed at how much taller I'd grown (I hadn't noticed) and told me Helena could take an hour to get home after school. "She and the girls must be window-shopping again. When you find her, could you please speed her on her way?"

"I'll do that," I said, certain I'd find her with Richard, not the girls. Partway along Secord Street, I saw her. And Richard. Together. Holding hands. I understood what made the walk home take so long. How had they escaped a busybody reporting them to Mrs. Pekkonen? They stopped in front of Richard's house.

When Helena spotted me, she squealed, "Saara!" and ran to embrace me.

I squeezed her in return. "I missed you heaps."

"Have you moved back home?" she asked, grinning.

"No, we're heading back to the farm today, as soon as we get the results of my aunt's checkup. The doctor's optimistic that she's no longer contagious."

"Terrific! I know you were worried."

"Hello, Saara," said Richard, offering his hand to shake.

"Hello, Richard." It felt awkward to have him behave like a grown-up. I wanted to tell Helena how close we'd come to losing Auntie, but not in front of Richard.

"Read that part of Gordon's letter to Saara, Richard." To me, she said, "You won't believe this."

He pulled a paper from his trousers pocket, unfolded it, and read, "*The Germans hit us with gas—a yellow-green cloud of deadly chlorine. Made my eyes water and burn. We were ordered to breathe through a piece of cloth soaked with our own piss …*" He glanced up to see my reaction.

I was shocked—and disgusted.

"I know, it sounds horrible, but the ones who obeyed orders survived," Richard explained, tucking the letter

back in his pocket. "The others all died from the gas."
Then he confided, "Gordon tells this kind of news only
to me. I have to hide his letters from my mother. The
ones she and Gordon's sweetheart get are completely
different."

Richard's eyes left my face and he blanched. Helena
and I followed his gaze to a uniformed lad on a bicycle
peddling toward us.

Helena clutched my arm. "It's the telegram boy."

He braked and propped the bicycle against the fence.
"Hello." Consulting the envelope in his hand, he asked,
"Is this the Williams residence?"

Richard nodded and accepted the telegram. Without
a word he strode into his house.

The telegram boy tipped his cap to us, mounted his
bicycle, and rode back the way he'd come.

In a panicky whisper, Helena said, "No telegram is
good news these days."

I trembled, hoping the news wouldn't mean a black
wreath on their door. "We'd better go."

Helena and I started walking home. At Bay Street,
hooves clopped behind us.

"Saara, climb up." It was Uncle Arvo. The team was
hauling a loaded wagon.

Giving Helena a hug, I told her, "Write to me when
you know Richard's news." I clambered up to sit next to
Uncle. "Goodbye."

All she could manage in return was a wave.

As we bumped along in the rolling wagon, Uncle's
eyebrows furrowed. "We must first stop at the doctor's

office and ..." His sentence trailed off and hung between us until he parked the wagon and handed me the reins. "You're in charge."

Less than five minutes later Uncle Arvo erupted from the doorway, grinning broadly. "Marja's not contagious anymore!"

I stood, threw my arms into the air, and shouted, "HURRAH!" Ace and Copper jerked the wagon forward, forcing me back onto the seat. Laughing, I tugged on the reins I'd forgotten I was holding. The team halted. Copper snorted and stamped her hooves in annoyance.

Uncle leaped aboard, grabbed the reins from me, and clucked to the team.

At my house, we dashed inside. Uncle embraced his wife and spun her around, whispering in her ear.

"I'm no longer infectious!" exclaimed Auntie, tearing off her mask. She turned to embrace Mama and Sanni, then me. "I want to shout it to the world!"

"Settle down, Marja," cautioned Uncle. "Dr. Koljonen said to be careful so you don't relapse—"

"I know, Arvo. But it doesn't hurt to celebrate, does it?" Auntie's face shone.

All the way through Port Arthur to the country road, Auntie held Sanni's little hand. When I offered to pass Sanni to her, she declined. "I don't trust my arms to hold her—she must weigh close to thirty pounds."

I'd grown so used to carrying her, she didn't feel heavy to me. A joy-bubble swelled inside me as I imagined how happy life at the farm would be with our biggest fear gone. I looked forward to sharing Auntie's wonderful news with Lila and her mother. If only there wasn't the troubling uncertainty of Richard's telegram.

The one-year anniversary of the *Empress* disaster was approaching. I expected my nightmares to intensify as the date neared. I dreaded the dark.

After settling Sanni for the night, I ran to the cabin to talk with Auntie about my fears. She continued to spend the nights there to ensure she got the rest she needed. I found her writing in my journal. "Oh, you're busy."

"Come in. I want you to read this." She handed me the journal.

"Are you sure?"

"Most definitely."

May 26, 1915

Rakas pikku Sanni,

You are a daisy springing up, blooming with life. I'm so happy because I've been feeling a great deal better and can help care for you. These times with you have been a joy. Yet when you come near and raise your arms to be lifted up, I cannot do it yet. You are such a heavy child that I must be careful. Saara is a capable little mother who makes sure you have plenty to eat. She is God's blessing to all of us in ways too numerous to count.

When I say good night and leave for the cabin, you come and lean your cheek on my knee or pat my face. In your clear baby voice you call me "Mama." I'm no longer a stranger to you. How wonderful this is to a mother's heart and makes me beg God to heal my body

completely—at times I shout so that He might hear my
prayer, because, as Saara convinced me, you do need your
mother.

With all my love,
Your mother

Auntie mopped her eyes. "Saara. Dear Saara. You've been a tremendous help to us. Day and night you've laboured without complaint." She stood and hugged me. "You've cared for Sanni the best you could and she has thrived."

Through my own tears I said, "I'm sorry for eavesdropping and reading your letters."

"You had no business doing that." Her eyes glistened. "But if you hadn't, I'm afraid—"

"I know it was wrong, and I promise never to do it again."

She hugged me again. "I'm so sorry I blamed you for what happened to Sanni."

I left grinning, having no wish to bring up my nightmares and spoil the happiness I felt at her forgiveness.

All day on May 28 I relived our voyage of one year ago. Auntie helped me prepare meals (anything she could do sitting down), but I was too keyed up to carry on a sensible conversation.

By the time Mr. Seppälä dropped off the mail after supper, I was as jittery as a skittish colt. There were good wishes from my family for my thirteenth birthday on Monday. But there was also a letter from Helena.

Dear Saara,

You asked me to tell you what the telegram said. The news is horrible beyond words. Gordon is dead. He was officially reported killed in action. I haven't stopped crying since Richard told me. He's pretending they're okay, but I can tell he and his parents are devastated.

Your best friend,
Helena

It was the news I'd feared most, yet I had to read her letter several times for the reality to sink in. My world listed like the deck of the sinking *Empress*. The faraway war pierced my heart. I shook as gooseflesh rippled along my arms.

Gordon was gone. He'd never tease Richard again. He wouldn't get married. I hadn't known him well, yet tears poured down my cheeks. To think, just on Tuesday I had heard how Gordon had survived the poison gas attack. Now, on Friday, we were mourning the loss of brother, son, beau, friend. How could I express how sorry I felt over their loss? No words seemed adequate, but I wrote them a letter.

The loss of Gordon made me see that my being at odds with Mikko was ridiculous. I had to put things right between us, but how? Grief and guilt weighed me down.

My dream that night was so powerful it convinced me I was back on the steamship. The starboard side of the *Empress of Ireland* burst open. River water poured in. The ship's siren wailed. My eyes opened in complete darkness; terror seized my throat. I had to get to the open deck. Wresting my tangled bedclothes from my legs, I charged toward the door.

Whack! My shin struck an object. The pain cleared away the remains of the dream. The siren's call transformed into a baby's cry. Sanni. My hands found her familiar shape. I nestled her up to my shoulder and fully awakened. Soothing her restored my normal breathing and calmed my fears. *Thank you, Bunny.* For once my nightmare was cut short, yet it still took ages to get back to sleep.

In the morning, I dragged myself out of bed. As I cooked the porridge, each sound from outdoors raised my hopes that it was Auntie coming for breakfast. When she arrived and raised her eyebrows at my droopy appearance, I poured out the news of Gordon's death and my memories of the horror-filled night when the *Empress* sank.

After I shared the worst of them, she embraced me. I sobbed. She crooned and stroked my hair. I felt the weight of all I'd struggled through begin to ease.

"Dearest Saara. You and I have faced terrible ordeals." She held me at arm's length and stared into my eyes. "It's been difficult for us to speak about them, but now I wonder if it's time to keep silence."

I mulled over her words, my lips still quivering.

Auntie continued, "I'm suggesting a pact between us, for the sake of our sanity. If you agree to never talk about the *Empress*, I'll never talk about tuberculosis. Shall we start a new chapter of our lives?"

"Will it stop these bad dreams?" I longed to be free of their heart-jolting terror.

Auntie slipped her arm around my shoulders. "There's no guarantee, but as my mother always says, 'You are the smith of your own happiness.' Whenever horrible memories come into our heads, we'll try to focus on our blessings instead."

Her words strengthened me. Perhaps I'd never need to speak or dream of the *Empress* again.

27

Auntie improved so much over the next couple of weeks that we began to talk about my returning home—perhaps after Juhannus, near the end of June. There was one thing I had to do before leaving. As I walked to Mikko's, I rehearsed my long-overdue apology to him.

Entering the barn, I hesitated. I'd forgotten the wording I'd practised.

Too late—Mikko spotted me. "Saara!"

A blush heated my face. "Mikko, there's something I want to say." My hands trembled so much, I had to set down the basket I was carrying. "I'm taking *pulla* to Fanni and your aunt, but I had to see you ..."

"Saara, it's all right—"

"No, Mikko, it isn't. I'm sincerely sorry for how I treated you after Sanni's fall. I was so scared and angry, I said things to you that I regret."

"At first what you said hurt. But the more I thought about how bad you were feeling, the more I understood." He stood the pitchfork he was holding against the wall and walked toward me. "You were right, it *was* a stupid idea on my part. For that, I've felt awful. I wanted to talk with you but wasn't sure you'd listen. I'm sorry for avoiding you all these weeks."

"Me, too. I don't want to lose you as my friend."

"I'm happy to hear that." His blue eyes lit up with his smile.

Relief and joy washed over me. Would I ever not blush when Mikko paid attention to me? "How is your foal?"

"Come see her for yourself." He motioned me into the stall.

The foal pressed against her mother, their coats an identical brown. The mare swished her tail to rid them both of pesky flies. I approached slowly and stroked the white blaze on the foal's face, saying, "She's a beauty." Like her mother's, each of the foal's legs below the knee was white, including the feather. The long hair partly hid her hooves.

"She'll fetch a good price," said Mikko.

"And then you'll buy your Canadian horse," I said.

Mikko nodded.

"I'm leaving after Juhannus, probably ... but I could give you an English lesson every day until then ..."

"Yes, please, Miss Mäki," he said in perfect English, with a grin.

After breakfast on June 24, Auntie sent me outdoors to check whether Uncle had decorated the entrance to the house for Juhannus. Birch saplings stood on either side of the doorway. "All done," I called.

My family was coming for that night's Midsummer

celebration, which would also act as my farewell and Sanni's first birthday party. Auntie didn't need full-time help to take care of Sanni and her farm duties any longer. Lila wanted to train to be a domestic, so she would help Auntie for part of each day. I'd go home in the morning, in time for the last week of school. As much as I wanted to return to my own life, part of me rebelled at leaving the farm.

My belongings were already packed. I'd decided to leave my silver spoon, hoping it would remind Auntie how much we all loved her. But that morning she'd plucked it from the sugar bowl, adamant that I take it with me.

A cloud of dust in the distance announced the arrival of my parents and brother. I stared at the small dark horse pulling the rented carriage. He looked too short to haul the load, yet he moved with ease.

"Hello," I called, sprinting across the farmyard. "I'll take care of the horse. What's his name?"

Papa set down the reins with a lighthearted laugh. "Canuck. I had to ask twice. Thought the man was only kidding."

Canuck—of course. It was obvious that he was one of the famed Canadian horses. I stroked his long, wavy mane before unhitching him from the buggy. Once his harness was removed, he was a breeze to groom, compared to Ace and Copper. I could see over his withers, so he couldn't have been more than fifteen hands high.

"There you go, Canuck," I said, forking hay into the manger of his temporary stall. I hated to leave him, but

I needed to return to the kitchen. I couldn't wait for Mikko to see him.

"It's time you got to work, miss," teased Mama. "I'll tackle the beets for the salad if you'll do the potatoes."

"That suits me," I said.

Auntie smiled. "Then I'll bake cardamom cookies."

We left for the party with Sanni wearing her harness and Auntie and Uncle holding her hands. John raced ahead. When the rest of us reached the Koskis' lake, we paused to admire its wind-rippled surface. The gathering brought all of our neighbours together.

"Saara," called Lila, beckoning me to the table weighed down with food (including strawberries!). "You've got to taste this." Why were John and Mikko snickering behind her? Lila popped a small meatball into my mouth. "What do you think? I made them myself."

I chewed the extra-spicy meat and swallowed, suppressing a cough. "I like the pepper." Lila grinned.

"Try using more meat than pepper," teased Mikko. Lila playfully punched his arm.

"Mikko, you have to see the horse my father hired," I said.

"Why?"

"He's a Canadian!"

Mikko hounded me with questions while we filled our plates and arranged ourselves on the blanketed lakeshore. The joyful conversation flowing around me had me laughing one moment, then feeling sad to be leaving the next.

After supper, John joined the younger boys for a game of tag. Sanni toddled to me, saying, "Awa, Awa." She pulled my arm, wanting me to play.

"Auntie, I'll watch Sanni so she can play in the sand," I offered.

"She'd love that," said Aunt Marja.

When I rose to go, Mikko said, "Do you mind if I come along?"

"I don't mind," I replied, blushing as usual.

Auntie whispered to Mama, "'Poverty and love are impossible to hide,' no?"

I turned my blazing cheeks away.

Near the water, Sanni gave up trying to walk in the unstable sand. She sat down and pounded a rock against an exposed tree root.

"Saara, I have something for you." Mikko pulled a paper-wrapped package from his trousers pocket and handed it to me. "I wish I could finish it. Fanni insisted I build new kitchen benches, so I ran out of time to make it exactly right before you have to leave."

Sanni grabbed at the paper, tearing off a piece. I finished unwrapping his gift. It was a small carved wooden horse: stocky, with a long, curly mane and tail.

"It's a Canadian, isn't it?" I said. He nodded. I ran my finger down the crest of its neck and across its back. "It's perfect. Thank you."

We strolled back to the picnic spot. Lila wore a wild-flower wreath and fashioned one for me. Uncle built the *kokko*, arranging the bonfire wood on a raft.

The sound of Mrs. Seppälä strumming her *kantele* set my feet tapping. After many songs and countless dances (yes, I danced with Mikko), Uncle declared, "It's dark enough to light the *kokko*."

When the bark on the birch logs above the blazing kindling ignited, he launched the bonfire raft. A ribbon of gold reflecting across the dark water linked the *kokko* with land. It was my favourite sight of Juhannus.

I felt Papa's hand on my shoulder. "All you've done for Arvo, Marja, and Sanni makes me a proud man. *Kyllä on*, Saara-*kulta*."

Yes, indeed, at that moment I felt like Saara-gold.

Auntie smiled and rocked her baby to sleep. Sanni had a real mother again. I looked around at the friends and family that I'd grown to know so well over these past months. To think, I could have chosen to play Aedgiva and rescue an imaginary prince. Instead I'd chosen to play myself, and unbelievably I'd rescued my beloved aunt. Could that be the reason I'd been spared? Perhaps it was only part of the reason. In my heart I felt a sense of purpose I'd never known before.

I caressed the Canadian horse in my pocket. Not knowing when I'd be back to North Branch, I harvested the images, tastes, and sounds of that special night and packed them into my memory jar. I intended to preserve them forever.

After my first day back at school, I started a letter to Aunt Marja:

Port Arthur, Ont.
June 28, 1915

Dear Auntie,

It feels good to be home. Please don't misunderstand me when I say I'm relieved to be done the housekeeping and looking after Sanni. It was harder work than I imagined it would be, but I wouldn't have wanted to miss the experience.

I was so disappointed not to see Miss Rodgers at school. She's in Toronto! Her brother was injured in a battle overseas and she left teaching to nurse him back to health. This war has cost so much, and now it's expected to last another whole year.

Thinking about Miss Rodgers reminded me of the decision I'd come to on the ride home from the farm.

Teaching English to Lila and Mikko showed me I want to become a qualified teacher. By the time I'm trained, I hope North Branch is big enough to have a school. If they hired me, I could teach Sanni!

I was reminded, too, of the essay about goals Miss Rodgers had asked us to write. She'd graded mine higher than it deserved. If I were to write it again now, after what I'd been through, my essay would be different—and better. As important as goals and dreams were, I realized it was far more important to *be* the kind of person who followed through on her promises. And who listened to her conscience and did the right thing.

In my bedroom that night, I pulled Canuck—the horse Mikko had carved for me—out of my pocket and caressed the perfectly formed face. Would my future include real Canadian horses? I smiled. If it did, I'd name the first colt Chief.

I stood Canuck on my dresser and thought of Mr. Blackwell's letter back in the top drawer. When he wrote, *Sarah, your life has been spared for a purpose*, he was right. My life was spared for a purpose—*on* purpose. I figured it was going to take me the rest of my days on earth to discover all the reasons why.

"Be quick, Aliisa," said Mom. "Mummu's already in bed."

I raced to my great-grandmother's room. Mummu was smoothing her multicoloured quilt over her legs. "*Kiitos*, Mummu." I kissed her forehead and breathed in the scent of her lilac perfume. "Thanks again for letting me have your *Empress* spoon."

"You're welcome. I'm so glad you think it's special."

"And you're special, too. I was wondering, did you ever get to be in a school play like *Aedgiva's Quest*?"

"No. I gave many recitations, but there were no plays." Then Mummu chuckled. "During my teacher's training I did get a role in a play at the Big Finn Hall. It was called *Tyhmä Jussi—Stupid Johnny*—and I teased my brother to no end."

I giggled. Sincerely I said, "I love hearing your stories, even the sad parts. Did Aunt Marja talk about her tuberculosis after she promised not to?"

"Oh, no—for her, that was a forbidden word. Auntie called that time the most sorrowful months of her life. She tried to forget it as much as she could."

"Aren't we always supposed to talk about stuff that upsets us?"

"Yes, that's probably better. But when I was young, people tried to pretend bad things never happened." Mummu set her glasses on the bedside table. "I remember when Auntie's first great-grandchild was born, she said, 'In those dark times I believed I wouldn't live to see Sanni grow up. Now to have a great-grandchild—I never thought life could be this good to us.'"

Mom poked her head into the room and said, "Time to go, Aliisa."

"But I haven't told her my news!"

Mom pointed to her watch and said, "You have thirty seconds—Mummu needs to go to sleep."

Excited all over again, I told Mummu about how my family and I had been discussing summer vacation plans.

"I found this website about the *Empress of Ireland*. There's a 3-D exhibit at a museum near Rimouski, close to where the ship sank," I explained. "So we're going to drive there and visit Montreal on the way back. When we come home, I can tell you all about it."

Mummu smiled and whispered, "*Kiitos*, Aliisa-*kulta*."

"Sleep well, Mummu," I said and gently hugged her.

On the way out I stopped at her dresser. I picked up Canuck, the horse that Mikko—Pappa—had carved for her. As I stroked the horse's smooth neck, I thought about Mummu's stories and our trip. I couldn't wait to get to Rimouski.

Before I closed Mummu's door, I peeked in for one more look at her. My heart felt heavy as I thought of her lost friend, Lucy-Jane Blackwell.

Like sun piercing the fog, an idea emerged. We could find a boat to take us to where the *Empress* still lay. There I'd throw a lilac sprig on the water in memory of Lucy-Jane.

One life lost—another lived on purpose.

Tuberculosis

Over the centuries, tuberculosis (TB) has been called "phthisis," "White Plague," and "consumption." TB is a bacterial infection caused by germs inhaled from the cough or sneeze of a person with active TB, or consumed in the unpasteurized milk of a cow with bovine TB.

During the early 1900s, tuberculosis killed more Canadians—one in seven—than famine or war or any other disease. Most families had at least one member suffering from this dreaded disease, considered a death sentence. Famous people who have died of tuberculosis include John Keats, Shawnandithit (the last of the Beothuks), Frédéric Chopin, Anton Chekhov, Gavrilo Princip, Jean de Brunhoff, and George Orwell.

Of the people diagnosed with contagious active TB, as many as possible were isolated in sanatoriums. They were given rest, plenty of nutritious food to eat, and lots of fresh air. This was called "taking the cure"—but it wasn't really a cure. That would have to wait until the discovery of bacteria-killing antibiotics. Before antibiotics, if patients recovered, it was because their own immune systems had successfully fought the TB bacillus, trapping it and walling it off.

The first Canadian sanatorium opened in 1897, and Toronto's sanatorium, the Toronto Free Hospital for Consumptive Poor, opened in Weston (now part of Toronto) in 1904. This facility changed names several times, becoming the Toronto Free Hospital for Consumptives in 1910 and the Toronto Hospital for Consumptives (also known as Weston Sanatorium) in 1924. It became renowned worldwide for research into and treatment of TB. Still, during the Toronto sanatorium's first twenty-five years, forty-five percent of the patients died.

A large percentage of tuberculosis patients in Ontario sanatoriums in the early 1900s were immigrants, many of whom contracted TB after arriving in Canada. TB patients in northwestern Ontario had to travel to Toronto to "take the cure" until 1935, when a sanatorium opened in Fort William. By 1938, there were sixty-one sanatoriums and dedicated tuberculosis units in hospitals across Canada. Sanatorium stays ranged from several months to several years. Surgical procedures were sometimes used to treat TB but were not guaranteed success.

Effective antibiotic treatment for TB was developed during the 1940s; after that, sanatorium treatment came to an end. Some sanatoriums, like the Toronto one, converted to general healthcare centres. Others simply closed their doors.

Today tuberculosis is a largely forgotten killer in North America, yet this wasting disease, at times in new, drug-resistant forms, is on the rise. One in three people worldwide carries the TB bacillus, and about ten percent of these people will develop active TB. More people die of TB today than at any time in history—1.5 million in 2006. In Toronto alone, there are approximately four hundred cases of active TB per year. TB is frequently present in association with HIV/AIDS; the very cells that are required to fight TB are the cells that the AIDS virus destroys.

Socialism

Many Europeans immigrating to Canada in the late 1800s and early 1900s were socialists. Under socialism, resources and industries are owned by the state or community instead of private individuals or businesses. Socialism promotes cooperation and fair sharing of wealth in order to make life better for everyone.

Socialists wanted to improve the lives of workers in Canada through higher wages and safer job sites. Together with other supporters of the labour movement, Finnish-Canadian socialists worked toward forming unions. Finns had a high degree of literacy and spread their ideas through their own newspapers. They organized Labour Day parades, demonstrations, and, at times, strikes. These actions often led to conflict with managers of the companies for which they worked (Finns were employed mainly in the construction, lumber, mining, and fishing industries). As Finnish-Canadian socialists became more radical and anti-religious, hostilities arose between them and the church in the Finnish community.

Finnish-Canadian socialist organizations throughout Canada established community halls, labour temples, and cooperative stores. They provided cultural and self-improvement opportunities such as drama societies, dances, sports clubs, and libraries.

Canada and the First World War

Fire from a spark,
war from a word.
—FINNISH PROVERB

In 1914, Europe was on the verge of war. The spark that ignited it was the June 28 shooting of Archduke Franz Ferdinand, next in line to the throne of Austria-Hungary. His killer was a nineteen-year-old Serbian named Gavrilo Princip. (An interesting note: Princip had tuberculosis.) Austro-Hungarians, believing Serbia had trained Princip, insisted on having a role in his prosecution. Serbia refused. On July 28, Austria-Hungary declared war on Serbia, and soon many nations were pulled in: Russia backed Serbia, and Germany declared war on Russia, then on Russia's ally, France. During the first week of August, Germany invaded Belgium, and Great Britain declared war on Germany. Then Canada entered the "Great War." This reduced a torrent of immigrants to a trickle; instead, a torrent of young men—more than one hundred thousand—rushed into Canadian recruitment offices to enlist. To them, the war was a grand adventure not to be missed. Thousands of women volunteered for overseas nursing duty, too. Predictions were that the fighting would be over by Christmas. Nobody imagined it would drag on for more than four years.

In February 1915, Canadian troops were established in the trenches of France. Their first major battle occurred on April 22, when they stopped a German attack at Ypres. It was also their introduction to Germany's large-scale use of an insidious new weapon: poison gas.

On the home front, in Canada, imported foods and clothing became scarce, which raised their prices sharply. People were asked to curb their consumption of meat. Factories were encouraged to produce munitions. The government Remount Purchaser scoured the country in search of suitable horses for the cavalry. Rumours of German spies in Canada were rampant; it was said they were planning to destroy key installations such as bridges, power plants, and radio stations.

Accurate reports of the fighting in Europe were not available initially. Canadian newspapers depicted the battles in optimistic generalizations. Eventually the official casualty lists began to paint a grim picture of horrendous destruction and loss of life. The "grand adventure" no longer held the same appeal. Black arm bands appeared in greater numbers. When hospitals in France and England ran out of room, injured Canadian soldiers were returned to Canada to recuperate. The most urgent need? Providing care for soldiers with tuberculosis.

Further Information

Tuberculosis

Invisible Enemies: Stories of Infectious Disease, by
    Jeanette Farrell

World Health Organization: www.who.int/tb/en

Stop TB: www.stoptb.org

Lung Association of Canada: www.lung.ca

Lung Association of Canada (history):
    www.lung.ca/tb/tbhistory

West Park Healthcare Centre (history):
    www.westpark.org/about/history.html

World Vision: www.worldvision.ca
    (click "Programs and Projects," then "International
    Programs," then "TB and HIV and AIDS")

Socialism

*The Penguin Book of Canadian Biography for Young
    Readers, Volume II, 1867–1945*, by Barbara Hehner
    (pages 176–188)

*The Journal of Otto Peltonen: A Finnish Immigrant,
    Hibbing, Minnesota, 1905* (My Name Is America
    series), by William Durbin

CBC Digital Archives: http://archives.cbc.ca/politics/
    parties_leaders/ (click "Tommy Douglas and the
    NDP")

Canada and the First World War

The Kids Book of Canada at War, by Elizabeth MacLeod

Library and Archives Canada:
    www.collectionscanada.gc.ca/firstworldwar/

Veterans Affairs Canada:
    www.vac-acc.gc.ca/remembers/
    www.vac-acc.gc.ca/youth/

Nose-blowing drill supervised by a Toronto school nurse (1913). —CITY OF TORONTO ARCHIVES, SERIES 372, SUB-SERIES 11, ITEM 62

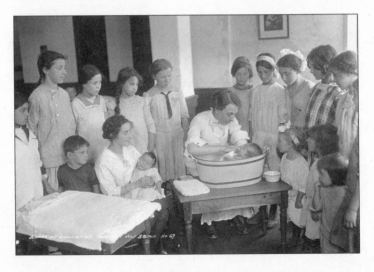

Little Mothers' Class in a Toronto school (1913). —CITY OF TORONTO ARCHIVES, SERIES 372, SUB-SERIES 11, ITEM 67

Mr. Otto Maki (author's great-grandfather) and infant Hilja Maki (author's paternal grandmother) held by her temporary caregiver, Mrs. Charles Salonen, in Nipigon, Ontario (1914).—COURTESY ANITA LANGE

Mrs. Aina Keto (foster mother to the author's paternal grandmother), Finnish immigrant farm wife on a homestead in northwestern Ontario (early 1900s). —COURTESY ANITA LANGE

Tuberculosis patient in a wicker rolling bed at the Fort Qu'Appelle Sanatorium, Saskatchewan (1920s). —COURTESY LUNG ASSOCIATION OF SASKATCHEWAN

Little patients of the Queen Mary Hospital for Tuberculous Children, Toronto (circa 1913).
—COURTESY WEST PARK HEALTHCARE CENTRE

Tuberculosis patients at the Toronto Free Hospital for Consumptive Poor "take the cure" in mid-winter (early 1900s). Exposure to the outdoors was a common treatment before antibiotics were developed. It was believed that replenishing affected lungs with fresh air would limit the spread of TB germs and encourage lungs to heal naturally.
—COURTESY WEST PARK HEALTHCARE CENTRE

A tuberculosis patient's living quarters inside a former horse-drawn streetcar generously provided by the Toronto Transit Commission. The photograph was taken at the Toronto Free Hospital for Consumptive Poor (early 1900s).
—COURTESY WEST PARK HEALTHCARE CENTRE

Postcard of the Queen Mary Hospital for Tuberculous Children, Toronto (1933), obtained by the author's maternal grandmother during her time as a patient in the Toronto Hospital for Consumptives.—COURTESY ANITA LANGE

GLOSSARY AND
PRONUNCIATION GUIDE

Note: As shown by the capital letters in the pronunciations, the emphasis is always on the first syllable in Finnish words. "K" in Finnish is a sound halfway between "k" and a hard "g"; in the guide below, it is represented by a "k" or a "c," depending on which makes the pronunciation clearer.

Hauskaa Joulua	HOUSE-caw YO-loo-uh Merry Christmas
Joulupukki	YO-loo-poo-kee Santa Claus
Juhannus	YOO-hahn-noose St. John's Day or Midsummer, a festival held on June 24 until 1955, when it was changed to the Saturday between June 20 and June 26
kantele	KON-te-le (the "e" sounds in "te-le" are the short "e" as in "let") a traditional Finnish folk instrument, originally with five strings and resembling a lap harp or zither
kiitos	KEE-tohss thank you

kiitos paljon	KEE-tohss BALL-yone thank you very much
kissa	KEES-sa cat
kokko	KO-ko bonfire
kulta	KOOL-tuh gold
kuutamo	KOO-tuh-moe moonlight
kyllä on	CUE-la OWN yes, indeed
leipä	LAY-pa bread
mämmi	MAM-mee traditional Finnish Easter dish of sweet dark brown rye-malt porridge
mummu	MOOM-moo grandmother
näkkileipä	NACK-ee-LAY-pa flat round rye bread, baked with a centre hole for threading onto a rod to dry, resulting in a thick crispbread
Onko täällä kilttejä lapsia?	OWN-ko TAAL-la KEEL-te-ya LUP- see-uh (the vowel sounds in "TAAL-la" are as in "cat"; the "e" in "te" is as in "let") Are there any nice children here?

pappa	BUP-puh grandfather
pulla	BOOL-uh sweet yeast bread flavoured with cardamom
rakas pikku	RUH-cuss BEEK-coo dearest little
sauna	SOW-nuh ("sow" rhymes with "how") Finnish steam bath
Tyhmä Jussi	TEWH-ma YOOS-ee ("ew" in "tewh" sounds like "ewe" and the "h" in "tewh" is emphasized; "ma" sounds like "ma" in "mat") Stupid Johnny
viili	VEE-lee processed sour whole milk with the consistency of yogurt
voi	VOY oh!
yhdeksän	EWH-dek-san ("ew" in "ewh" sounds like "ewe," and the "h" in "ewh" is emphasized) nine

ACKNOWLEDGEMENTS

Thank you to the Okanagan Regional Library staff; Ilkka Koskivuo and Kyllikki (Cookie) Dampier for help with Finnish language questions; Derek Grout for information regarding the *Empress of Ireland*; Alice Jensen, registered clinical counsellor, for insights about post-traumatic stress and survivor guilt; Jeremiah Wiebe for John's note; Laurie Molstad and Margaret Rosati for providing a retreat for writing; Lyyli Repo and Holly Williams for information about Finnish immigrant life; Tyyne Marja-aho and Esteri Ylinen for their childhood memories; my grandmother Hilja Lange for her memoirs of life on a Finnish immigrant farm; Andy Ruoho for his memories of living at my great-grandfather's homestead; Beverly Soloway for research into Port Arthur life in 1914 and 1915; Diane Hunley, RN, and her consultants for information about tuberculosis diagnosis and treatment in Port Arthur in 1914 and 1915; Vince Rice, director of public relations at West Park Healthcare Centre, for reviewing the manuscript for accuracy regarding the Toronto Free Hospital for Consumptives; Kathryn Bridge for reviewing the manuscript for historical accuracy; and

Jean Morrison and Mark Charlton for reviewing the socialism section of the historical note.

I am grateful to Fiona Bayrock, Helen Berarducci, Eileen Holland, Sue Noble, Kathy Pelletier, and Nikki Tate for their encouragement and help at various stages in creating this book; to student reviewers April Kieke and Cameron Waller for their valuable feedback on the manuscript; and to Brynn Tucker for modelling as Saara. Heartfelt thanks to Patricia Fraser and Loraine Kemp for thoughtfully critiquing the entire manuscript, and to Mary Ann Thompson for in-depth manuscript critiques that elevated my writing to another level.

To my parents, Art and Anita Lange, many thanks for helping with details of Finnish-Canadian life, translating Mummu's letters, reviewing the manuscript, and constructing the pronunciation guide. To my husband, Will, an enthusiastic first audience of my writing, and my children, Annaliis and Stefan, huge thanks for being ever supportive and encouraging. I want to thank Diane Morriss for her support for the story idea from the start and her confidence in me; Laura Peetoom and Dawn Loewen for their editing skills that strengthened the story; Jim Brennan for his book design; and Frances Hunter for her skilled layout work. Lastly, special thanks to Aili and Eino Ala—Mummu and Pappa—for both the shared and the never-spoken-of parts of their life stories, especially Mummu's battle with tuberculosis and letters to her infant daughter, which inspired me to explore how tuberculosis affected Canadians in the early 1900s.

Karen Autio holding the
water bucket of a dip-well at
the Father Pandosy Mission
in Kelowna, B.C.
—WILL AUTIO PHOTO

When **Karen Autio** asked her Finnish-Canadian grandparents to record their life stories, she was given a glimpse
of her grandmother's brave yet mysterious battle against
tuberculosis as a young mother. The idea for *Saara's Passage*
took tangible shape after Karen read letters written by her
grandmother to her infant daughter, Karen's mother, letters that were discovered after her grandmother's death.

Saara's Passage is a sequel to *Second Watch* (Sono Nis
Press, 2005), Karen's historical novel inspired by the tale
of a silver spoon from her grandmother and the wreck of
the *Empress of Ireland* steamship in 1914. *Second Watch* was
nominated for the Chocolate Lily Award and has been
enthusiastically received by children, teachers, reviewers,
and parents.

Like many Canadians of Finnish descent, Karen grew
up in the Thunder Bay area. She now lives in Kelowna,
British Columbia, with her husband and two children.
To learn more about Karen Autio and her books, visit
www.karenautio.com.